The Priest

About the Author

Nainette Rayner has been widowed for sixteen years. She lives alone and her main interest is gardening, with ½ an acre of her own it has to be!

Having studied for two years, she achieved her RHS certificate at the age of seventy-six and wondered what she should turn to next. Nainette read about the creative writing group in the local press and as she enjoyed writing letters and the recipients tell her they loved reading them, she decided to join and *The Priest* is the result.

Recently, Nainette found a steamy love story written in an old school exercise book when she was aged twelve - perhaps there was some latent talent, it has just taken a while to develop. She is now eighty-eight years old.

Nainette Rayner

The Priest

Olympia Publishers
London

www.olympiapublishers.com
OLYMPIA PAPERBACK EDITION

A CIP catalogue record for this title is
available from the British Library.

ISBN: 978 1 84897 677 1

First Published in 2016

Olympia Publishers
60 Cannon Street
London
EC4N 6NP

Printed in Great Britain

Dedication

For Oenone

Acknowledgments

With huge gratitude to my friends at the Hayes, Kent Creative Writing Group – for their interest and ongoing encouragement.

Chapter One

The road wound upwards, stretching out towards the sunset, all golden and tranquil. It was only when one rounded the corner however, that the smell became apparent – not as a scent nor an aroma wafting on the still evening air but something much harsher and invasive, polluting the atmosphere that retained warmth from the blistering sun of the day on that Aegean coast.

The dry, hot surface, sand and shale underfoot, scuffed by her sandals, sifted up between her bare toes – occasionally a sharp flint bit into them and she shook it out and flicked it into the sparse growth that struggled between rocky outcrops where small lizards scuttled, settling beneath their shade for the night after sunning themselves all day on their flat, warm ledges. Here her nostrils were titillated by the strong perfume of the herbs, marjoram and thyme, that the locals gathered to flavour their cooking and the small, pale irises' sweeter hints. But over and above these as she walked on, was the smell.

A positive stink was assailing her now – what on earth? Then she saw the cloud of flies darting and buzzing above a patch of bare ground over beyond the next bend of the road.

A sudden gust of chill wind blowing off the sea which lay spread out below, shimmering in the diminishing light, made her pull her shawl more tightly across her shoulders as she stopped and pondered whether to investigate – it was probably some dead animal that had lain some time, putrefying; perhaps, poor thing, it had crawled up here to die and was now making a meal for the flies that engorged on its blood. Then she heard a dog bark close by and a wild looking mongrel burst round the corner and came racing toward her. It started to follow her but she waved it away.

Her heart thumping, the girl started warily across the intervening scrub, placing her feet carefully between the rocks. She waved her arms at the flies and screwed up her eyes against them, batting them away from her head and face. Looking down she saw first a scrap of material but then made out a tiny foot projecting from where it had been wrapped around a little leg. At the other end of the bundle, a thin wisp of golden hair – a few black flies still entangled in it, curled over the edge of the cloth and she saw it was a small infant lying face down, dried blood on its scalp.

She felt sick but reached out and gently rolled her find over and found herself looking into the soil-caked, swollen features of a baby; the cloth shifted away from either side of its body and she saw that it still had the umbilical cord uncut and bloody hanging from its wizened belly and glistening white, fat maggots bored into the flesh. Choking and retching, she took off her shawl, gathered up the pathetic little cadaver and wrapped the shawl protectively around it.

Hugging her bundle close to her, the girl stepped back from the place where it had lain amongst the rocks and scrubby patch of scree. Her shawl masked the worst of the deathly smell that came from the abandoned body. She pulled it close to hide the sad little infant's face and wondered what she should do next.

There was a path, she remembered, just a few yards ahead, that led steeply down to a quiet cove on the seashore. There wouldn't be anyone there now in the cooling evening and she would be able to wash the baby's body in the sea before planning her next move.

At the top of the cliff path, when she came to it, there was a wayside shrine. She saw that a posy of wild flowers had been laid there at the feet of the plaster Madonna. The blooms looked fairly fresh, the petals of the wild cyclamen still retained their pink and magenta tones and a diminutive wild iris still gave off its delicate scent.

The girl crossed herself and murmured a prayer, "Ave Maria, bless this child," she interceded also for the poor mother who had needed to abandon it up here.

Then she started downwards, stumbling and catching at the clumps of stunted vegetation on either side of the ill-defined path, to steady herself. At last the path opened out and she stepped onto the sand. The tide was nearly in so she hadn't far to walk before she could lay down her burden. Her feet were scratched and bleeding and she kicked off her sandals and paddled into the water to soothe them before returning to the baby.

Once again she bent to unwrap its tiny form from her shawl and then carried it to the water's edge. She laid it where the waves were lapping gently and unwound the material that was sticking to the bloodied limbs. Carefully she splashed the cleansing salty water onto the face and cleared the nose and mouth. She bathed the eyelids and untangled the dead flies from the golden hair. Next she washed around the child's belly, wishing she had something to cut away the birth cord and laying it between the parted legs which revealed that this was a boychild.

One of the baby's fists, she then noted as she turned to wash his arms, was clasped tightly around something. Very gently she prised apart the perfectly formed fingers with their exquisite miniature pearly nails; on the palm of the hand lay something that glinted in the last rays of the evening sun. She held it up and wiped it with the edge of the winding cloth – it was a gold crucifix still with a broken piece of chain slotted through it. She put it carefully into the pocket of her skirt and finished her task of cleaning the little boy.

The young priest hurried along the coast road, his soutane billowing out behind him, blown by the rising onshore breeze. Below the cliff the setting sun sparkled the sea in rosy ripples stretching inland from the horizon – deep shadows crept up the sides of the square, flaking, whitewashed single storey adobe houses set along the broken paving, scrawny chickens pecked at the weeds coming up between the cracks and in and around the open doors, hoping for scraps.

The young man kept his head bent and seemed oblivious to the greetings called to him from doorways. A grizzled old man came towards him leading two goats on frayed rope bridles, he pulled off his cap and crossed himself as the priest drew level but there was no response to his gesture.

The houses became less crowded together and the paving ran onto a dusty baked-earth path; on either side the patchy scrub grew more dense; the scents of wild oregano and thyme grew stronger, carried on the breeze as the priest scurried on. He was muttering agitatedly under his breath, his fingers pulled at the crucifix he wore hanging on a leather thong from around his neck – "Mea culpa, mea culpa," he whispered.

He arrived at the top of the cliff path that led down to the little rocky inlet beneath, and paused. The sea, glimpsed through the tangled branches of rosemary and stunted pine that straddled the way down, lapped gently at the shoreline. As he watched, he noticed a movement below, a young woman was there, seemingly washing some clothing in the shallows at the water's edge; he wondered how she had got down there and would she come up on this path – he didn't want to meet anyone – he craved solitude in which to contemplate his problems. He looked around for somewhere to sit and sank down on a smooth rock, his head in his hands.

This is where the young woman found him.

"Father, I was coming to see you." She held out the bundle she was cradling in her arms. "What am I to do? I found him back there lying at the side of the road."

The young priest looked up then got to his feet.

"I washed his poor little body down there on the beach. Who could have abandoned him?" the girl continued, "Oh, and he had this in his fist." She transferred the infant to one arm while she reached into the pocket of her skirt and took out a tiny gold crucifix and broken chain. The priest took it from her and examined it closely, turning it over in his palm. There was an inscription on the back of the cross, he made out the name – Christina.

"Oh my God, my God," he cried aloud, "This belongs to a young woman in the village, she was pregnant, she wasn't married, she felt she had shamed her family and left them. I don't know how she managed or where she found shelter, this child must be hers." He leaned forward and took the infant from the girl. He held it tenderly close to him stroking the fine, blond hair. "A little boy. Oh Lord a son, forgive me Lord." The priest burst into tears, racking sobs shook his thin frame and the girl looked on horrified, unable to move to console him.

"Please Father—"

Chapter Two

The boy progressed along the wide, sandy beach, sometimes running or jumping, darting in and out of the breaking waves at the edge, sometimes stopping to pick his way carefully over the rocky outcrops and pausing to linger by the small pools captured in them, poking gently between the gleaming pebbles, teasing out the tiny crabs that scuttled beneath them, with a piece of gnarled and twisted driftwood, bleached almost white by the salt and sun. He laughed aloud as he played his solitary games, searching further behind the strand at the base of the cliffs edge where long-fallen rocks lay and occasionally gave up their treasure of scrolled ammonites from long centuries past.

His straw-coloured hair tangled in the on-shore breeze, his tanned limbs and bare, sand coated toes spoke of long days spent in the sunshine, it was the school holiday before his last term there and he revelled in the freedom. Soon he would have to give it all up when he started at the seminary in the autumn, which would lead to him taking holy orders and following the career his parents had planned for him. The eldest of five boys and three girls, it was his destiny to enter the priesthood.

The local priest, Father O'Doherty had confirmed him as a young child and recruited him as a server at the village church's alter. Now he was sixteen years old and had to give up childish things and knuckle down to his studies. He was a good student, applying himself to the learning of Latin and Greek and had exemplary results in his examinations. He looked forward to the new subject of theology. The kindly priest encouraged him all along the way, perhaps seeing in the eager, happy youth, his own young self. The life of the church had suited the old man. He enjoyed his own company and his books and had not found the vow of celibacy difficult to adhere to. He had come to this small parish on the east coast of Eire after his first curacy in the Dublin suburbs some twenty years earlier and having served in several positions in town parishes, he enjoyed the slower pace of life in the village, the wide seashore and sky, the light and shade on the ever-shifting waves. Whenever he could get away from his pastoral duties he would come down to the beach and walk along it, bundling his soutane up into his belt and doffing his cap so he could feel the wind blow through his remaining wisps of grey hair. His keen blue eyes took in everything about him. He had studied the guide books and could recognise each different species of seabird, the raucous seagulls and the dainty oyster catchers pecking at the tiny grey shrimps and green algae. He had taught the boy all he knew and together they collected weirdly, sea sculpted, driftwood and delicate shells or hammered for ammonites in the ancient rockfalls.

Anthony was a handsome boy, his sisters' friends and all the village girls found him very attractive. He had danced with them sometimes at Feast Day celebrations and they admired his strong, long strokes when he swam in the sea. Their mothers too were drawn to him, recognising his qualities of good manners and bearing as well as his good looks. Some of them were heard to mutter "What a waste, him going into the church when he might have made a fine husband for someone." But after he began at the seminary and was seen less often in the village, the women all followed his progress with interest and when he visited home, enjoyed his charming smile and greetings for each of them.

After his five years in the seminary and his ordination, Anthony was sent to Dublin to serve in his first curacy as had his mentor, Father O'Doherty, in his time, but he had ambitions to travel and when the opportunity arose for him to take up a position in one of the scattered islands in the Aegean by a small Christian community, Anthony didn't hesitate and soon found himself, Father Antoni in a seaside village not unlike the one he had been brought up in. The sea was bluer, the winds gentler, the air was warmer and scented with wild herbs and the perfume of the spreading cyclamen and tiny narcissus growing along the cliff top and the crevices of the cliff face, and the sunsets were far more glorious, great swathes of crimson and gold lining the darkening sky before giving way to glittering starlight.

He soon settled in his new surroundings, the diocese gave him a tiny, whitewashed cabin for his home, furnished sparsely with peasant-style chairs, a table and slatted wooden bed with a colourful patchwork spread across it and his carved ebony crucifix on the wall at its head. A village woman, Eleni, came every day to clean and cook for him, sweeping the stone-flagged floor with a witch broom and preparing good, plain peasant food served on heavy terracotta plates with fruit and local wine. Often he found a posy of wild flowers in a jug on the table. He had his work, his books and the seashore for his walks and Anthony was content.

His duties were not arduous, the usual regular services and saint's day celebrations, christenings, confirmations, funerals and a few weddings. The incumbent priest was a lazy cleric and more than happy to delegate to young Father Antoni so that he himself could enjoy his wine and his siestas in the long, hot afternoons in the cool shade of the manse behind the half-closed shutters or in his garden, stretched out on a wooden bench beneath a great bay tree that was intertwined with a burgeoning pink bougainvillea.

Anthony called on the older parishioners after his lunch, taking them communion or simply chatting to them. He had soon picked up modern Greek patois from his classics studies and before evensong would stroll in the surrounding countryside or down on the beach where he would gaze out over the water in the vague direction of Eire, comparing in his mind the island coves with those of his childhood explorations.

Different fish were landed from the colourful boats of the local fishing fleets. Ugly, gaping jawed creatures that he had never seen before, many coloured octopus and large silvered sardines. He became accustomed to their new flavours, fresh from the nets, before they were packed in woven willow creels and taken to the markets; cooked by his housekeeper on the open hearth or served up in the village café and, on summer evenings, barbecued on the beach. Anthony didn't attend many of these beach parties, he felt incongruous in his dark clerical attire and assumed people would feel constrained in his company when the bouzoukis played and the village girls and boys danced in the firelight's glow and splashed wildly in the gentle surf.

The girls were joined in their admiration of the new Father Antoni, his handsome good looks, blond and blue eyed which was unusual in the local boys. They managed to come upon him often, crossing themselves and greeting him, calling him by name and delighting in his smiling response. They would go on their way, leaning and laughing together, discussing his charms and noting every wave in his fair hair and his elegant, long fingers.

A single cock's crow broke into Anthony's sleep. Mumbling to himself, he burrowed into his pillow but soon other cocks joined the first, echoing their monotonous calls around the countryside from farms and smallholdings to the yards where single cocks held sway over a clutch of domestic hens, kept for their daily lay of eggs for the family and on feast days, roasted for the table.

Anthony tossed irritably on his bed. He looked at the clock on the table beside it - four am. He recited his morning prayers early, but it helped him ignore the cacophony of the raucous dawn chorus of cock crows, interceding at the conclusion of the set texts – a plea for the blessing of a few more hours sleep and gradually, as one by one the cockerels throttled their fading cries, he fell back into a half conscious doze.

When he awoke again, it was altogether silent, too silent. He listened for the usual morning sounds. The swish, swish of Eleni's broom over the stone-flagged kitchen floor. The thud of mats being energetically banged against the trunk of the old catalpa tree in the yard. There was none of this, nor any clatter of dishes and pans and the gush of water from the taps as his breakfast was prepared.

He looked again at the clock, checking the time. It showed the correct hour for this domestic activity to have begun. He pushed back the hot, crumpled sheet and stepped out onto the sheepskin rug by the bed. After briefly splashing water, already warm in the ewer, before he poured it into the large, white basin, he dressed, picking out a crisp, white shirt from the chest, freshly laundered and ironed, that Eleni had brought with the rest of his washing the day before. She insisted on taking his personal laundry to her home to wash, feeling it was unseemly to have the priest's shirts, and underwear especially, flapping on the line in his yard, this was reserved for table linen and towels.

Going through into the kitchen, Anthony found the empty cup from last night's bedtime chocolate, unwashed and still on the table where he had left it. The flowers in the stoneware jug beside it, fading and drooping. The egg basket was empty but there was fruit in the bowl. He cleared away the cup and faded flowers, leaving them on the scrubbed wooden draining board by the deep stone sink and then, taking an orange from the bowl, he squeezed it, twisting the fluted olivewood juicer to let the last drop of liquid fall into a thick glass tumbler. He drank, standing by the stove while a kettle boiled. He found a small, round loaf in the bread crock and butter, rich and creamy, in the little refrigerator, with half a jug of milk.

Anthony laid all this on the table and set to brew his tea in an old brown teapot. Usually he had fresh ground coffee to start his day and he missed the sound of the grinder and the aroma of the beans, but tea was quicker and less trouble. He said his grace and then, as he spread his bread liberally with butter and rich, deeply golden honey, scented with wild flowers, he heard footsteps on the path outside and a young woman appeared in the doorway. She murmured an apology, explaining that Eleni was unable to come to work and had asked her to come instead. She was Eleni's granddaughter and she would be able to do everything that her grandmother did for him.

Anthony stood up and went to help the girl with the bags of provisions she had brought with her. He asked her name, Christina. She told him in near perfect English that Eleni's legs were badly swollen and that she had become very breathless. The doctor had been sent for. Then she shyly intimated that Anthony should finish his breakfast. He declined her offer of an egg and she took the broom and dusters and went to start work on the other rooms.

She was a quiet, shy girl but when she was going about her household tasks, sweeping and dusting and shaking out the mats and hanging his bedclothes out to air in the yard, she often sang to herself. She had a pleasant voice and favoured the local folk songs that Anthony recognised having heard them often, accompanied by bouzoukis at the village gatherings and beach barbecues. She collected his clothes and took them to be laundered as her grandmother had, bringing back his shirts dazzling white and crisply ironed and folded and laid them in the old, carved wooden press in his bedroom.

Emboldened as the days ran into weeks, Christina began to ask who were the people in the photographs on his bedside table – his mother and his brothers and sisters, laughing and playful in happy family groups and more formally posed and serious at his ordination in Derry Cathedral with dear old Father Doherty. His mother had written recently to tell him of the old priest's death and Anthony was glad to have his picture, reminding him of the days he had spent with the old man and the gentle guidance he had given him in his studies. Anthony was briefly touched with homesickness as he named his siblings in the photographs, one by one, to Christina. Ireland seemed so very far away, remote in its windswept, misted landscapes, so different from the bright sunlight and warmth of his present surroundings.

Christina began to learn the names of these far off strangers in the photographs. Pointing to them one by one and struggling with their Irish names; Maeve, Siobhan, Ruagh. Anthony wrote them down for her and though Christina spoke fairly good English learned from the nuns who ran the small village school, she was not able to read it and the Irish spelling couldn't easily be rendered phonetically – she and Anthony would be reduced to helpless laughter as she stumbled over the sounds.

Eleni seemed to be making very slow progress. She was now mainly confined to her chair. Christina set this out for her grandmother on the flagstones outside her open front door, where she could watch the passers-by and exchange greetings and the latest village gossip with them.

Anthony called on her in the course of his parochial duties and would bring a second chair from the house and sit beside her, watching her gnarled, brown fingers busily crossing and re-crossing the brightly painted and carved bobbins on her pillow, gradually revealing the intricate patterns of the lace she was working. He would refresh the water in the carafe set beside her on a small wooden milking stool, or bring her an extra shawl from inside if a cooling breeze blew up from the shore.

The old lady appreciated these little kindnesses and surveyed him keenly with her bright, black eyes. She saw how the sun had tanned his skin to deep gold, contrasting with his fine, bleached blond hair and she thought how this handsome young man would appear to her granddaughter. Christina's olive skin, her lithe young figure and long wavy, glossy black hair would surely be hard for Father Anthoni to ignore, yet his calling and long training in the catholic seminary in Ireland insisted that he remain celibate for life. Eleni wondered if this was really necessary. Young men who entered the priesthood and indeed the young nuns who came to teach in school, should surely enjoy the full opportunities that life could offer them. Wouldn't a loving God want that for them and wouldn't their priests be better able, with wider experience, to understand and assist with the problems and difficulties that their parishioners confided to them in the confessional.

As the year wore on and the days shortened, the Gregal blew in from the sea, fluffing up the feathers of the few chickens who still pecked about for scraps.

Eleni no longer ventured out onto her doorstep but instead sat by her window indoors watching over the comings and goings of her neighbours. Her granddaughter stayed with her, the rest of her family, her brothers and sisters, lived up in the hills above the village, working the harsh land to produce vegetables and a few vines and olives. In the spring, the almond trees blossomed in drifts of pink and white, all over the hillside; the sweet nuts were gathered in the autumn when too, the olive trees were shaken to loosen the sharp-flavoured green fruits.

Father Anthoni continued to call on her and give her the news of the parish and the world beyond. The old lady noted how Christina would tuck a flower in her hair when she went to the priest's house and shake her plaits freeing her long dark waves to spread out over her shoulders and down her back almost to her waist.

The sun still shone strongly in clear blue skies and the sea rolled, deeper blue into the shore, but it was time to see to the doors and shutters and look out warmer clothing for the winter to come.

Anthony loved the changing scenery and the crisper feel in the air, more like it felt in Eire. Christina now brought him the new season's honey and olives and she made warming soups in the big, black, iron pot in his kitchen. The villagers presented him with a new sheepskin rug and he found knitted gloves and scarves left shyly at his door.

Chapter Three

Gradually, Christina had persuaded her youthful employer to overcome his inhibitions and join with the local people in their beach barbecues and festivals. At first he was drawn into the dancing by the other young men of the village, linking arms with them and joining their waving line. He performed awkwardly, his black cassock flapping around his ankles, its high collar constricting his throat as the pace of the dance grew more and more wild and in time he left aside his vestments and came attired as the others, in jeans and shirt, the sleeves rolled up and the collar thrown open, displaying the crucifix at his chest. At first the girls were shy with him but each of them wanted to dance with the handsome young priest; they took extra care with their colourful dresses and wore flowers in their hair and, in the height of summer, when the wine was flowing and the voices loud with song and chatter, Anthony ran with the other young men headlong into the sea and splashed and ducked them with the same happy and reckless abandon, recalling memories of beach picnics with his school friends and sparring with them in cooler, Irish waves. Slowly the elders gathered up their baskets and shawls. The older men carried the kitchen chairs they had brought down to sit more comfortably on the beach and made their way back to the village calling "Goodnight" to each other and warning the youngsters not to be too late getting home. There was work to be done in the morning.

The young men came out of the sea and drew in a circle around the fragrant, dying embers of their barbecues, drying their clothes in the remaining heat and emptying the last of the bottles and jars of wine. The young girls slid closer across and leant against them in the moonlight. The sand was silvered and the ripples on the water glittered and danced in the soft, night-time breeze.

When the fire finally crumbled, collapsing until only a small heap of ashes remained, one of the young men took an empty wine jug and filled it with seawater from the edge of the shore and brought it back to throw over the ashes, which sizzled and sank, smoking, then he kicked some sand over the site and everyone gathered up their wine bottles and jugs and the girls their shawls and in ones and twos, the company made their separate ways up off the beach and with laughter and cries of "Goodnight", went back to the village. Anthony found himself alongside Christina and offered to accompany her back to Eleni's house as it was not far out of his way and they walked together, quietly talking of the evening's pleasures. He left her at the little white painted, lopsided, wooden gate at the end of Eleni's path, briefly taking her hand and she thanking him for the companionship.

Anthony turned and made his way back to his own home. He felt a small sense of arousal and it disturbed him. He let himself into the small adobe house, brushing past the frangipani bush by the door, releasing its sweet, heady scent. He went straight through to his bedroom, austere with its whitewashed walls adorned only by the black wooden crucifix hanging above the narrow bed, a few family photographs on the bookcase and a small table where his Bible and missal rested and papers pertaining to parish business. He undressed and went into the kitchen to splash some lukewarm water from the tap at the sink, over his head and face then went back to kneel by his bed and say his evening prayers. He prayed for guidance in his growing relationship with Christina and he decided he could not put it off any longer. He must make his confession about this to his superior, the parish priest, the next day. He got into bed and lay back picturing Christina, her lovely face and deep-set eyes, her soft long hair and her lithe brown limbs as he had sat near her at the barbecue, until he finally fell asleep.

Chapter Four

Father Giorgio was reading, sitting out on the little verandah at the back of the priest's house. It was still very warm during these early autumn days though the nights were drawing in and the temperature fell rapidly after dark. He slapped irritably at a mosquito buzzing around his head and shook his book to push it away, nearly knocking over the glass of wine that stood at his elbow on a small, rusting, wrought-iron table. He had done his parochial rounds this morning and now was ready to while away the rest of the day until evening mass, reading and relaxing in the afternoon sun.

Father Giorgio had been priest to the village for – he could barely remember how many years – the life suited him. Its easy tempo and regular seasons; children he had christened were now coming to him to make preparation for their marriages and he supposed he would be baptising their children in time and would, no doubt, be officiating at several funerals.

He himself had accepted his celibacy without difficulty, had never contemplated marrying. He had taken part – if from a distance – in the local village life but had never felt drawn to any forbidden relationship. Now his young curate had asked to come to see him and to hear his confession and Giorgio could guess the content of the latter. Antoni was a handsome lad and Giorgio saw how the village girls looked across at him during the services in church and blushed as they received the communion wafers from him, and their hands trembled as they held them out to the goblet of communion wine.

The verandah door opened and Father Antoni came out, ducking beneath the low lintel and apologising for entering through the house, explaining that he had found the front door open. Father Giorgio waived aside the younger man's excuses and motioned him to bring close the chair that stood at the other end of the verandah. He wanted this meeting to be informal and not conducted in the enclosed space of the confessional in the church. He was a shrewd observer of the life around him in the parish and had already discussed with Eleni her fears for her granddaughter and he was well aware of his responsibilities in guiding and directing the probationer chaplain in his calling. But it could wait a bit, they could chat a while. Discuss perhaps the books they were each currently reading.

Giorgio was an avid consumer of thrillers. He liked to work out the clues and discuss the red herrings spread through their texts and outwit their detectives. His bookshelves were filled with well-thumbed, lurid paperbacks – far outnumbering the religious volumes alongside them. He had recently acquired a second-hand computer from a visiting church office suppliers, had taught himself how to use it and was now able to order fresh titles on the internet. He laid down his present novel and sat back to give his whole attention to Antoni.

He listened to the stumbling account of the young man's innermost feelings in respect of a young woman of the village. No particular name was mentioned but it was clear that he was referring to his young housekeeper and Giorgio saw how troubled it made him. Christina was a beautiful girl, it would indeed be hard to resist the temptations that the church so rigidly demanded their clergy ignored. Secretly Giorgio felt that it should move on with the times and look more leniently on their priests and allow them to make relationships and lasting commitments sanctified by holy matrimony. How much better would they then be able, by experience – himself included – to advise on the problems of married life and difficulties between married couples, the anxieties of childbirth and the upbringing of their children.

Father Giorgio sat further back in his old, sun-bleached wicker chair, he worked his shoulders, settling them into the cushions behind him, the old chair creaking sympathetically. He usually enjoyed his siesta at this time with his book and his wine but he must try to help the earnest and troubled young man before him.

What could he say? He reminded him of the sanctity of the vows he had taken when he had begun his training in the seminary back in Ireland, then it had seemed easy along with his fellow students, before they reached their full manhood and had to face the temptations of the wider world and he implored him to consider the consequences should he enter into any relationship with a young woman, however innocent, not only to himself but to her also and her family. Had he made any declaration of his feelings for her, Giorgio asked. Anthony assured his confessor that he had not, but it was obvious to the older priest that the young man was agonising over keeping silent.

They spent a long time sitting there together in the afternoon sun, while the shadow of the catalpa tree lengthened and began to filter the rays that fell across the verandah. Father Giorgio confided his own early struggles with the problem Anthony was presently experiencing, reassuring him that as time passed one came to terms with one's avowed obligations to the priesthood and accepted celibacy. Finally, his advice to him was to pray for guidance for himself and to pray too for the young woman concerned. He got up from his chair, signalling the end of the interview and went with Anthony to see him out. They crossed the somewhat Spartan bachelor sitting room, bookshelves lined the whitewashed walls and piled onto a large mahogany desk amongst piles of papers scattered there and where Father Giorgio's recently acquired computer sat incongruously amidst the room's old-fashioned surroundings. Some religious paintings hung above the fireplace and a few statuettes of the saints stood on the heavy wooden mantelshelf. There were two worn, comfortable armchairs set either side of the open hearth, threadbare tapestry cushions sagging upon them and several faded, hooked rugs were laid about the flagstone floor. With a brief blessing and a promise to pray for him, the priest waved Anthony off and stood watching him walking slowly away, head bent, lost in thought, fingering his crucifix and seeing only the ground before him.

Father Giorgio went back to the verandah and finished his interrupted glass of wine; it would be time soon to prepare for mass. He sat for a while wondering what more he could do for Anthony. The lad had been in the curacy for more than a year now, maybe it was time for him to take a break, a time in retreat to think, away from the village and the problems of balancing his religious and social responsibilities there. Father Giorgio decided to speak to his superior and to seek a respite place for Anthony in the monastery at the further end of the island – a secluded and peaceful setting in the hills where the young priest could find solace and support from the monks in solving his difficulties, while joining them in their strict observance of the regular regime of masses throughout the day and night and helping with their chores in the house and the large, productive kitchen gardens and olive orchards that surrounded their ancient dormitories and cloisters. He retrieved his empty glass and, gathering up the cushions from the chairs, went inside, determined to write without further delay to the bishop and put his plan into operation. He poured himself another glass of wine – he needed a drink to help him concentrate on the letter he must write – and took it over to his desk. Sitting down, he opened a drawer and selected a thick, white sheet of paper from it, embossed with the insignia of Saint Gregory, the patron saint of the village church. He spread the paper on the ink-blotched blotter before him and picked up his pen. He sat scratching his forehead before starting to write.

Christmas was approaching ever more swiftly and there were many extra services to arrange. Father Giorgio searched the vestry cupboards looking for the nativity models, the sweet faced, blue clad Mary and her swarthy, bearded Joseph. The animals – some of them earless and tailless, the wooden manger still stuffed with last year's straw and the infant Jesus, rather larger than life size compared with his stiff, wooden parents. The children loved the nativity tableau and crowded round to touch the well-known characters of the Christmas story as they were displayed before the altar in the old church and they prepared excitedly with the nuns in their school to put on their own nativity play, delighting all the parents and grandparents who watched their performance, perched uncomfortably on the kindergarten chairs ranged before a small stage in the village hall. Their mothers conjured costumes from old sheets and angel wings from net curtains stiffened with sugar water starch and chicken wire, and a variety of home-made haloes adorned the children's heads, some sporting strands of tinsel that were brought out every Christmas to sparkle in the candlelight.

Birds were being fattened for the Christmas feast and traditional Christmas cakes and pies were taken to the bakers to be fired in his large brick oven.

Anthony threw himself energetically into the festive plans, forgetting his problems for the time as he helped the villagers put up their decorations in the church – wreaths of butcher's broom instead of the holly that would be picked to fashion them back home in Ireland, and vibrant crimson poinsettias filled the vases around the base of the lectern and the pulpit. He thought it would be quite acceptable and appropriate to give Christina a small gift to mark the season and as a thank you for her care of his house and himself through the past months, so he went into town one morning after Matins, hitching a ride with one of the local farmers who was taking some pigs to market, snorting and sniffing in the back of his ancient mud-splattered truck. A gaudily painted Madonna hung from the mottled rear-view mirror above the windscreen, swaying crazily back and forth with every rut and bend in the road.

Antony alighted by the market and walked on into the street of small shops where he found a jewellers. He chose a small gold crucifix and chain for Christina and had the jeweller engrave her name on the back of the cross.

It was nearly Christmas and Christina was going to her family on Christmas Eve, with Eleni. Her brother would collect them in his van after delivering live poultry to the market; feathers and straw would be all over the rear, where Christina would have to travel, Eleni having pride of place on the well-worn front seat which would be less dusty and smelly.

She had made everything ready for Anthony, giving an extra polish to his few pieces of furniture and setting a pot of poinsettias on the kitchen table. She had made him good, heartening, peasant stew for his supper which would last him for several more days – it sat in a big iron pot on the stove, simmering gently. She came to say goodbye to Anthony. He asked her to wait for a moment and went through to his bedroom to take a small jewel box from the drawer of his bedside table. He carried this back to where Christina was standing and shyly held it out to her. Christina looked surprised and eyed him enquiringly as he motioned that she should open the little box.

Christina gave a cry of delight when she saw the crucifix laid on a blue velvet cushion in the base of the box. She slowly lifted it up, turning it around and seeing her name on the reverse. She looked about her for somewhere to put the box and Anthony took it from her. As he was clad in his off-duty wear of open neck shirt and jeans, he put it in the pocket of these.

Christina meanwhile was putting on the necklace, fumbling with the clasp of the chain behind her neck. She appealed to Anthony to assist her and as she turned her back to him, she handed him the ends of the chain and swept up her hair, pulling the tresses across one shoulder and bending her neck forward, exposing her smooth, olive-skinned nape.

Anthony's hands were trembling as he took hold of the chain and clipped the ends of the fastener together then – he leaned forward and kissed the dear curve of Christina's skin and smelled the fall of her hair over his hand and stroked it, breathing in her scent. She turned to him and, looking up into his face with her large luminous dark eyes, their lips met and they kissed. Anthony felt the hot rush of blood to his head and he could feel his heart beating wildly. He seemed to be in an ecstatic spin and they kissed again and again, caressing each other's bodies and clinging together, went into the bedroom, Anthony half carrying the girl and laying her gently on his bed.

Later, their passion spent, Christina looked over at the young man beside her. He was sleeping as many young men will after the excitement of their first love-making. He lay with one bronzed arm flung out over the rumpled covers, looking so vulnerable and innocent. The afternoon was cooling now and he must soon awaken. Christina moved carefully so as not to disturb him and slipped from the bed, picking up her clothes from the floor and dressing hurriedly. She hadn't yet fully appreciated the enormity of what they had done – the priest and the village girl – and she left the house quietly, closing the door tightly, perhaps thinking in some way to protect Anthony from the condemnation of the local people, which should surely follow if her and Anthony's adventure was discovered.

The last of the Christmas masses had been completed and the next morning, early, Anthony packed a small case with a few shirts and underclothes, his missal and Bible, the former a gift from his old confessor and friend, Father O'Doherty, and one photograph only, of his mother, to take with him on his retreat.

He had spent half the night on his knees by his bed, the very scene of his madness, praying for guidance and forgiveness and for Christina, for whom he had been totally responsible, leading her into lying with him and giving herself to him, totally and innocently.

He left the house without breakfast, stumbling rather blindly first to the little church, cold and stark in the early morning. He laid down his case in the porch and pushed open the heavy, iron-studded, wooden door which was always left unlocked, and made his way up the nave. The nativity tableau, with its crib and carved wooden figures would be left in front of the altar until Epiphany, when the nuns, once again, would dust them and wrap them to put away in the vestry cupboards until the next Christmas. A smell of melted wax pervaded the air, coming from the burnt out stumps of candles which had blazed in their sconces the evening before and were now reduced to encrusted stalactite drips around their bases – another task for the nuns who would later peel them free and polish again the intricate metalwork stands and holders, and lay ready a new box of fresh, white offerings.

Anthony crossed himself and knelt, and then prostrated himself full length on the cold, tiled floor before the altar. Penitent and ashamed, weeping, he prayed again, feeling cast out. He should, he knew, make confession to Father Giorgio, but he excused himself that there was no time for this, he had to meet the local bus at the end of the village which would take him part of the way to the retreat house in the hilltop monastery across the island.

He rose to his feet, brushing down his cassock and drawing his warm, winter cloak around him. He wiped his tear-stained face, genuflected to the altar and made his way back to the porch to collect his suitcase. Slamming the door behind him, he felt he was shutting himself off entirely from the church and his life within it.

Though it was still early, the village was coming awake, the cocks crowed lustily, there was a clatter of pails as goats were gathered for milking; smells of baking bread wafted from many outdoor brick stoves that heated the surrounding area and brought chickens close around them, feathers fluffed up, eagerly pecking at the hot crumbs as loaves were pulled from the shelves. The strong aroma of coffee too, titillated his nostrils as Anthony strode along. One or two of the villagers greeted him and wished him well – Father Giorgio had announced his leaving, temporarily, to visit the monastery. Some offered him coffee, which he declined. He had no time to stop – one pressed a bag of fresh olives on him and he tucked this into the pocket of his cloak, muttering his thanks and blessing the giver.

As he approached the small, paved square where he would pick up the bus, Anthony saw that Father Giorgio had arrived there before him. He was sitting on a stone bench by the small municipal well beneath now almost leafless trees. A thin, grey donkey was tethered to one of these, head hanging, while its owner – an equally thin and grey old man – grappled with the chain to lower a bucket into the well to draw water for his charge. Anthony stopped, ready to offer his assistance but the chain suddenly rattled free and the bucket began its descend. The old man nodded to him and Anthony crossed to where Father Giorgio was waiting.

The older man had made some effort to meet Anthony. He wasn't used to early rising and liked to take his time, normally eating a good breakfast, but this morning he had left his house before his housekeeper had prepared it, gulping down only a cup of coffee to warm himself against the early morning chill. Now he stood up and opened his arms to embrace Anthony, his keen eyes taking in the troubled gaze that returned his own. He took the young man's case and motioned him to sit down beside him on the cold bench. There would be a few more minutes before the bus was due.

Father Giorgio sought to reassure Anthony of the welcome that awaited him from the brothers at the monastery and the peaceful opportunity there to deal with the problems that had been troubling him. He handed Anthony a letter, asking him to deliver it to one of the brothers with whom he, Giorgio, had shared studies in the seminary many years before. "We followed different paths, but we still maintain a tenuous contact," he explained.

Then a rumbling was heard and in a few minutes an ancient motorbus drove into the square and came to a stuttering halt. There were already a few passengers aboard, all warmly dressed for the early winter morning weather; some clutching boxes of vegetables, others steadying wicker baskets on their laps, from which issued squawking and cackling, luckless chickens, all on their way to market in the town.

The driver of the bus leaned out from his cab, a toothless grin across his deeply tanned face, his eyes almost disappearing in the crinkled furrows of his forehead. He greeted the two

37

priests as they came forward, urging them to take their time getting aboard, there was no hurry. Anthony climbed up the two deep steps at the entrance and turned to take his case from Father Giorgio. Then he walked back to take his seat by a window from where he finally waved to the older priest who saluted him in return, a hand raised in blessing. Now the driver wrenched the elderly gear lever into position and with a cough and a lurch the bus started forward, all its occupants keeping themselves upright, holding on to their baggages and the backs of the seats in front of them. The odd turnip falling from a vegetable box onto the floor where it rolled about until its owner managed to retrieve it from under one of the opposite seats, rather bruised and dented, and restored it to its box.

The various religious icons and garishly painted ornaments strung up above the windscreen banged and bounced with the staccato rhythm of the engine. A strand of Christmas tinsel hung down from the rear-view mirror – it must have impeded the driver's vision but he seemed unperturbed by it – brushing it aside only occasionally as the journey proceeded.

Anthony thus began on a long route ahead of him, jolting over the badly rutted road through several small hamlets where more passenger came aboard with their produce and livestock, even a small kid was allowed on after much coaxing and prodding from the young lad holding its bridle, its little hooves slipping and clattering on the unfamiliar steps and floor

Chapter Five

Anthony carried on having regular talks with the Friar in the library, when the sun was at its highest, Anthony experienced doubts, seeking for answers to them. The daily life in the monastery enfolded him in its routine and security and sometimes he thought that perhaps this was an option he could pursue for life – but he wondered if he could really make the complete break from his family in Ireland which would be required, he missed them all and their happy, rowdy times together and he had planned to go back to visit them some time soon.

There was no pressure put upon him to join the brotherhood but he couldn't help being impressed by their unwavering acceptance of their vows of poverty and obedience and their devotion to their timetable of prayers through night and day. The atmosphere within the monastery buildings and the surrounding gardens and vineyard was so peaceful and the men seemed so contented – he wondered about their families, how much contact they were able to keep between them; had they had girlfriends, or experienced the wonderful joy of holding one in their arms and giving of themselves one to the other? He couldn't put Christina out of his mind, the image and scent of her were with him every hour.

His stay at the monastery couldn't last more than a few weeks longer, then he would have to go back to the village and resume his parochial duties and see Christina again. How would their relationship be resumed, could it ever be innocent and platonic again? If he stayed here in the monastery all that could be avoided but he felt it would be cowardly not to see her again even if he did decide to enter an enclosed order, and he wanted to see Father Giorgio who had arranged this retreat for him and had understood so well his unspoken dilemma. The bell was ringing for prayers again and Anthony made his way there slowly, clutching his crucifix until his knuckles went white with the tightness of his grip.

Ariadne was near her time, she was heavy and tired now but excited too. Her mother and Eleni had decided the Christina should go back to the village to be with her, to help with the first weeks after the child was born. Eleni had grown a little stronger and assured Christina that she could manage without her, and she gave her the shawl she had knitted, painfully with her arthritic fingers, to take to Ariadne to wrap her great-grandchild in.

So Christina and one of her brothers drove in the old farm truck laden with gifts for Ariadne and the baby and fresh produce from the smallholding, down from the hills by the winding, rutted and puddled road to the little house in the village. Christina was impressed by the changes there, the smart new paintwork, the pots of geraniums and poinsettias bright against the freshly whitewashed walls and the new, brightly patterned curtains in the windows.

Stavros came in from work – making new carved pew ends for the church – to greet Christina and her brother and poured them wine to take with thick slices of bread that Ariadne had baked that morning, spread with dark honey.

Christina went to help Ariadne in the kitchen after being taken on a tour of the house and to view the tiny nursery prepared for the new baby. Christina would sleep on a divan in the living room during her stay, covered with a heavy, embroidered quilt that now lay folded on it and with cushions covered with material left over from the curtains Ariadne had sewn for the windows here and at Anthony's house. Christina, seeing these, couldn't imagine how they would fit with the austere surroundings of the young priest's home, they were too vividly coloured and strongly patterned.

The regime at the monastery was strict. Every few hours throughout the day and night there were calls to prayer and it was difficult to go back to sleep between the night-time masses and the daily routine of work was hard. There were goats to be fed and milked twice a day, calling them in from the pasture and teasing out the bales of hay to supplement their diet of the scant winter grazing, and rows of vegetables to be weeded and hoed. Anthony was given a coarse woollen habit and stout boots to wear when engaged on these outdoor jobs. His hands soon became calloused with his efforts and pulling turnips and other root crops from the cold, hard ground strained his wrists and arm muscles with the unaccustomed toil and the roughness of his borrowed habit had scratched and itched his exposed skin.

He took his turn in the household tasks, sweeping wind-blown leaves from the cloisters and polishing the pews and altar furniture in the chapel; the tiled floor needed washing daily and Anthony drew pails of water from the well and mopped them, restoring the vibrant colours that were dulled by the scuffing, dusty sandaled feet of the monks. He had to help in the kitchen too, burnishing the heavy saucepans until they gleamed, and scouring the wooden tables there and in the refectory that were worn and bevelled through use over centuries. The cooking was done over vast open ranges and bread was baked in enclosed brick ovens, the loaves removed with long handled, flat wooden spades, scorched by years of use. Olivewood ladles and spoons hung above the stoves on blackened iron hooks and piles of logs were stacked alongside, cut and collected by the monks from the surrounding wooded hills.

Everyone helped with the preparation of their simple meals, chopping and peeling vegetables and mixing and shaping pasta dough. Meat and fish appeared only occasionally on the table. There was a well-stocked pond in the grounds to supply freshwater fish and sometimes wicker creels of generous harvests landed from the fishing boats far down on the seashore, would be brought up the steep road to the monastery by donkey and were served then and some salted in tubs for future meals. There was fruit and olives from the orchards and wine that the monks made from the grapes in their vineyards under the direction of the master vintners of their order and stored in great wooden casks in the vaults beneath the main building.

Anthony enjoyed his work in the herb garden with its rich aromas of oregano and thyme, the feathery foliage of fennel and the sharp scent of lemon balm that stayed on his habit and hands. He had little time to ponder his problems though they were never far from his mind and his personal prayers.

He had delivered the letter from Gorgios to his friend at the monastery, wondering how much, if any, information about his relationship with Christina it contained, and the elderly friar sought him out to talk with him in the library; this was a handsome room stocked with shelves of leather bound religious works and furnished with tooled leather-topped desks for the monks to study at in their periods of rest from their chores. Conversation among them was limited during the day to afternoon rest and recreation periods and, when necessary, in the grounds, but only to facilitate the work there. The goatherds murmured gently and encouragingly to the animals, leaning their heads against the creatures' warm flanks as they milked them – and an occasional expletive was heard when a hoe struck hard rock, followed by an apologetic plea for forgiveness for the fault and quiet laughter among the nearby brothers who had heard it.

Up in the hills above the village, Christina was a welcome pair of hands. Eleni was now very frail and it had been decided that she should stay within the family and that Christina too should remain and continue to care for her grandmother as well as help on the smallholding. One of her sisters, Ariadne, had recently married and Eleni was happy to give over her little house to Ariadne and her husband. He was a carpenter by trade and would be able to find work around the neighbourhood. They were delighted with the offer and moved in straight away. Stavros soon had the lopsided wooden gate hanging straight and freshly painted and Ariadne planted up the various terracotta pots and jars around the small yard, with herbs and spring bulbs. They whitewashed the flaking walls and painted the door and window frames and inside, repaired and repainted the old lady's small rooms and few pieces of furniture. Ariadne was pregnant and lovingly began decorating one tiny room for the baby and she knitted coverlets for the cot that Stavros had begun to make. They restored the old hen house at the back of the house and re-stocked it with four chickens, looking forward to having fresh eggs from them, in time.

Anthony's house was still empty awaiting his return and Ariadne made a few visits there to keep it aired and dusted as Christina had asked her to do. She loved looking at the photographs of his Irish family that Christina had described to her and took the opportunity to take down the curtains and replace them with new, brightly patterned ones that she made while sewing her own for her new home and Stavros helped her hang them. She was pleased with the effect and hoped Christina's priest would like them.

Chapter Six

Christina had had a happy childhood, playing in the hills among the olive groves and the orchards that clad the slopes in a haze of pink blossom in spring. Her's was a hardworking family, every member had to take their turn at the hoeing and weeding of the vegetables that struggled through the stony soil and harvesting them and helping with the seasonal pruning of the olive trees and the ranks of vines. From an early age she had learnt to feed the chickens and collect their eggs, carrying these carefully in her small hands, and to milk the feisty tethered goats, leaning her small weight against their sides and avoiding their horns. She couldn't carry the full buckets to the house, one of her older brothers did this until she was older and could take their weight.

She soon became stronger and her skin darkened in the summer sun and it was time for her to go down to the convent school. She'd run barefoot mostly until then but when she set off to walk the two miles to the convent, hair tightly braided in two plaits and wearing a white blouse and black tunic – a little too big for her – she wore white socks and gleaming, black, polished leather shoes. She felt both confined and proud in her uniform and enjoyed seeing her blouse flapping on the washing line in the yard every day, dazzling white in the sunshine; her shoes thrown off as soon as she had trudged home, dusty and scratched, were lovingly polished by her father when he came in from his work on the farm and Christina, her bare toes released from them and her socks, felt them curl and feel the grass between them, her braids already with wisps of hair escaping from them by the end of the school day, were unplaited and fell around her shoulders, thick and glossy.

She was a good student and attended the nun's school regularly for some years, missing classes only when she was needed at home at sowing and planting and harvest time. At fourteen she gave up schooling altogether and worked full time in the house helping her mother with the cooking and cleaning and doing her chores with the animals, the goats and the donkey who worked the wheel at the well and pulled the cart loaded with tools and composted vine and olive prunings to the furthest edges of the small farmstead. In autumn there were olives to be shaken down from the trees and gathered for pressing, their oil collected in wooden casks, and grapes to be picked and crushed to ferment and brew into wine.

The stone barns around the house were lined with wooden shelves supporting bottles of oil and wine and round goat cheeses maturing in their crinkled white crusts. Every corner was suffused with their combined scents. Eggs preserved in jars and tomatoes bottled or made into pastes and sauces made a colourful display. The chickens skittered across the straw on the earthen barn floor, sheltering from the winds in winter and the blistering summer heat.

At holiday times, Christina would go down to the village to stay a few days with her grandmother and enjoy the seaside. Eleni would pack picnics in a big wicker basket, a bright chequered cloth tucked around generously buttered hunks of freshly baked bread, with cheese, and they would make their way down to the beach, picking their way along the rocky paths scented with wild thyme and oregano that flowered between the boulders on either side. Eleni was younger then and wiry, her thin, muscled, brown legs and strong feet taking her easily on the descent and up again at the end of the day when the picnic was lighter and Christina gave her a hand to hold.

Eleni would paddle at the water's edge, her black skirt bunched up around her hips, extolling the virtues of salt water for her feet and then she would find a rock to sit beside, leaning her back against its warmth and would bring out some embroidery or lace-making, teaching Christina the intricacies of the craft, though the girl had been taught plain sewing and mending and some threadwork by the nuns.

Together they would pick samphire to make into soup and find small crabs in the pools between the rocks, left after the tide had receded, to have for their supper.

Eleni delighted in her youngest grandchild, entering into her imaginative games and sharing her joy of discovery of the seashore; the tangle of seaweeds and the tiny creatures that lived among them; the brightly coloured sea anemones clamped to the rocks, ceaselessly waving their tentacles like underwater flower petals. When they'd had their lunch, Christina shook out the crumbs from the cloth and the gulls came, squawking and jostling to pick them up and strutted close looking for more, so that Eleni flapped the cloth at them and Christina, laughing, chased them off into the sea.

Christina made patterns on the sand with seaweed fronds, pink, yellow and green and scored her name with a stick, watching it fade gradually as the incoming tide gently pulsed over it, until it disappeared altogether.

And far away, where the tides lapped a distant shore – a flaxen haired boy splashed and swam in cooler waves and spelt out Anthony on the sand.

Chapter Seven

Anthony had thrown himself wholeheartedly into the life of the monastery, carrying out all the tasks allotted him with good humour and to the very best of his endeavours, bearing cheerfully the scratching of the loaned habit and the scars from the sharp flints and snapping twigs from the gardening. Now the friar looked at him with some admiration. Father Giorgios had respected the confidentiality of the confessional and not made any mention of the specific problems his young curate struggled with, that had led to his bishop sanctioning this period of retreat and he could only approach Anthony through discussing his faith in general.

There were few tourists in summer who made their way up to the monastery, to wonder at the paintings and icons preserved there from long times past and there were some communicants who came on short retreats who enjoyed the peaceful tranquillity within, that gave them some time to look into their souls more objectively than was perhaps possible in their day-to-day lives. Nikos, the friar, would sometimes meet the fishermen and some other suppliers of necessities to the monastery that the monks could not produce themselves, though they were almost completely self-sufficient.

He acknowledged that it took a different kind of man to renounce all outside human contact, family and friends to devote his whole life to prayer and service to a higher authority, but he valued his long-standing, fragile friendship with Giorgio who had followed a different course and probably a more practical one.

Surrounded by books, the two men talked together about their favourite authors and Anthony marvelled at some of the old, bound manuscripts that Nikos took down from the shelves to show him, meticulously illustrated and coloured by monks of past generations of the order.

Both men were well-read and their conversation was lively as they exchanged views but at this first meeting they didn't have time to touch on Anthony's reasons for being there, before the Great Bell rang for the next call to chapel and they both dutifully made their way there through the vast colonnaded cloisters, joining the brothers coming in from the gardens, wiping their hands on the hessian aprons they were untying as they walked along and exchanging their boots for sandals that they had left ready.

The soft drone of the recited office and the music of the sung liturgy were soothing to Anthony and he felt uplifted and, for the moment, forgetful of his predicament. Nikos had arranged that they should meet again in the library the following day to resume their conversation.

In the solitude of Anthony's temporary cell – its bare, whitewashed walls devoid of any decoration save for a wooden crucifix and sparsely furnished with a narrow wooden bed and stool. Two black hooks on one wall provided hanging space for his few clothes and an iron sconce holding two white candles provided lighting. His mother's photograph he propped on top of his small suitcase. The floor was plain terracotta tiled and a mat of rushes by the bed saved his bare feet from meeting the chill of the floor when he got up in the morning and during the nightly calls to prayer, and was his only kneeler when he prayed alone.

So busy and organised were his days that though he thought of Christina often, he couldn't concentrate his mind on what had happened between them and what were the consequences. Sometimes he argued with himself that one act of indiscretion – albeit a physical one – couldn't possibly lead to pregnancy, could it? He recalled their slight fumbling coitus – for both of them it was their first – yet it was a sublime moment; with eyes closed he recalled it, the closeness of their bodies, their scent, the wonderful loving gaze of Christina's beautiful eyes looking up at him and drawing him into them, his own heart beating wildly, the gentle touch of her fingers across his back. How could it be wrong to enjoy this wonderful experience. To have vowed never to indulge it, could that be right? Until he fell asleep, his mind raced round and round, offering no comfort or solution.

Christina, up in the hills, was confused. She too was kept very busy helping on the family smallholding as well as caring for Eleni. She shared the room and the big old bed that she had shared with her sister, with the old lady and was often disturbed more than once during the night to tend her. It was hard to get back to sleep; Eleni's snoring was irritating and though Christina gently tried to shift her grandmother to stop it, Eleni soon fell over on her back and the deep snoring began again.

As she lay awake, Christina thought of Anthony and their brief partnering in the narrow bed in his home in the village. Ariadne had been back to collect more of her and Stavros' things and she had described the new curtains she had made for Anthony's windows – giving Christina a sharp stab of jealousy and regret that she had not thought of doing this herself.

Christina's jobs around the small farmstead included caring for new-born calves, she was awed as she observed each birth and helped up the tiny, slippery creatures, wiping them free of their cauls and massaging them to stimulate their breathing and setting them upright on their splayed legs in the soiled and trampled straw. She took her turn in the vegetable rows, weeding and hoeing and gathering the crops and helping her mother prepare and cook them for the big family meals.

It was a few weeks since she and Anthony had left the village and Christina tried to put her anxieties of what they might have caused by their love making to the back of her mind, but eventually she could no longer ignore the signs and she withdrew into herself, there was no one she could confide in, she knew what her parents' reaction would be and she wasn't aware of Eleni's views of priestly celibacy and felt she would have no sympathy for her granddaughter's predicament. So she worked on, keeping her growing secret to herself. She was a strong and healthy young woman and wasn't affected by any side effects experienced by many of her peers in the early stages of child bearing. It was difficult to make contact with Anthony at the far end of the island and she longed for him to be allowed back to the village when she might get down there with one of her brothers to see him.

Christina enjoyed being back in the village, she was welcomed there by her young friends and the older residents too. Some of the older women glanced at her quizzically, but though she was now all of three months pregnant, her more rounded figure was attributed to the healthy outdoor life she had been living up in the hills with her family and the work she had been doing on their smallholding. She herself felt the gently swelling of her abdomen with a mixture of terror and anticipation of what was to come and she stroked its new curve with the beginnings of love for the tiny creature carried within it. She watched Ariadne, now awkward and clumsy, her rolling

51

gait and her tiredness and wondered how it would be for herself as her own time drew near. She tried to ignore the implications of her situation and considered if she could ever come to share her fears with Anthony.

He, after his stay at the monastery, had asked for leave to go home to visit his family in Ireland; he wanted more time to consider his future course and needed to have them around him to decide whether he could possibly give up all contact with them should he decide on a monastic life. He had travelled directly from that secure establishment and so had not seen Christina before he left but he would soon enough be back to take up his curacy, if that was to be his choice and then, he assumed, Christina would be cleaning and cooking for him and there would be new parameters to be set about their relationship.

Christina now went to his house and kept it aired and dusted, the curtains that Ariadne had made for his windows, Christina had to admit, certainly brought a new brightness into the rather stark rooms and she set about adding little touches of her own to them, bringing in small ornaments and colourful linen table cloths and towels. Following Ariadne's example, she planted pots of geraniums and tumbling purple hibiscus in the little yard and she found a figurine of St Theresa to stand by the street door.

She felt that it must be time to make her confession to Father Giorgio but she kept putting this off. She didn't know how much that gentle old man knew of her relationship with Anthony and indeed, Anthony too did not know yet of her pregnancy.

It would soon be Easter and there would be much going on in the church. Anthony would be returned by then and be busy with extra masses and celebrations, they wouldn't have much time together and Christina had to find somewhere to live in the village if she was to continue working for Anthony, or go back to her family and caring for Eleni. Either prospect frightened her for it couldn't be much longer before her pregnancy was evident and there would be talk. She must protect Anthony and couldn't name him as the father of her child though she longed to share their secret. There seemed no one she could confide in.

Anthony was welcomed so warmly back into the loving circle of his family, it was as if he had never been away. He discarded his sombre priestly garb and revelled in the opportunity to being just himself, not revered for his calling nor treated any differently, but only as the elder brother.

Spring in that part of Ireland was a lovely time. Inland, the countryside was burgeoning into bloom; clouds of white blackthorn blossom flourished in the hedgerows, tiny wild daffodils nodded their yellow bonnets beneath them, trembling in the gentle breezes and celandines starred the roadside banks with their glossy petals shining amongst the fresh green ferns and mosses.

Anthony walked the lanes and shore, sometimes with his younger brothers and sisters but more often he made his way alone to the beach and walked there along the strand for miles. The on-shore wind cleared his head of the thoughts that troubled him as he strode past the fallen rocks from the cliffs and skirted the tangled seaweed margins of the constant pounding breakers. He loved it all, the tangy, salt-laden air, the crashing of the waves, the scudding grey clouds tiered overhead. He watched the wheeling white winged gulls beneath them, swooping down occasionally to dive for a fish, or to land, bold and bright ringed eyed, so much bigger than they seemed on the wing, mincing along the firm, wet sand with their staccato gait, pecking at shrimps and small sea creatures washed in, in the yellow, frothing spume, with their large beaks.

Now and then he came upon an ancient curled ammonite impressed in a boulder and tried to prise it free with a piece of driftwood but this always shattered and he threw it away, flinging it as far as he could into the sea. He thought of old Father Doherty and smiled at remembering their shared fossil hunting expeditions and their easy companionship, a time when Anthony had no doubts about his future career. He also found time to go to Dublin and meet up with his sister Maura, who was in her first year at Trinity; she'd been a bright pupil at school and had won a bursary to the university to study history and art, with a view to a future in teaching. Together she and Anthony walked in the Great Library and pored over the Book of Kells, marvelling at the intricate calligraphy and brightly coloured illumination of the texts produced by the medieval monks. They strolled through the city parks and along the banks of the Liffey, enjoying their brief reunion and sharing their news. Anthony didn't confide any of his problems to her but simply enjoyed her company, finding her much grown up since he'd last seen her.

His mother saw a change in him though and worried for him. Anthony had always been close to her and he tried to answer truthfully all the questions about his life in the church overseas. The younger children wanted to know about the sunshine and swimming in the warm sea and the beach parties and barbecues, and his father, who had always been a shy and taciturn man, now that his first born son had grown to manhood and entered the priesthood, found him hard to talk to though he was proud of him in his chosen career.

Upstairs in his bedroom at night – a younger brother had moved out of it, not without protestation so that Anthony had it to himself – he wondered what the family's reaction would be if they found out about his forbidden relationship with Christina.

Eleni eased herself slowly, with a deep sigh, onto the old, high backed wooden chair set out beneath the shade of the ancient, gnarled vine which wounds its way, heavy with clusters of ripening purple grapes, beneath the beams above the loggia along the back wall of the farmhouse. The sun was high and burned down on the parched fields and orchards beyond but here there was some respite from its fierce heat and the old flagstones were cool beneath her feet. She shook off her shoes and spread her toes against the stone, feeling their relief. Her hands lay, unusually for her, folded in her lap; her fingers were becoming increasingly bent and swollen and she could no longer work the intricate lace that used to occupy her every resting moment. She'd been helping in the house all morning, sweeping and dusting and in the kitchen making the fresh pasts for the family's midday meal, peeling fresh picked tomatoes and crushing garlic for the sauce. Now everything had been cleared away, the great pans scoured and burnished and the plates neatly stacked on the cupboard shelves along with the spoons and forks, and Eleni felt she had earned this quiet time just to sit and watch the thin blue line of the sea, sparkling far off below the mountains and the workers in the sun-grilled fields, and beneath the grey-green foliage of the olive groves, moving slowly and deliberately between the furrows and branches, hoeing, weeding and pruning.

She was thinking about her granddaughter, Christina. Eleni had watched the girl and noted the slow rounding of her belly, quickening now, it couldn't be hidden for much longer. She knew a little how Christina would be feeling, her own first-born child had been conceived before her marriage, her parents and the rest of the family had been ashamed by and for her, and she had been pushed into hastily arranged wedlock. Old Father Giorgios had been the young curate in the village then; Eleni remembered his shyness and his sympathy for her, he would surely feel the same sympathy for Christina's plight, but he too would guess who was the father of this child and how would he be able to reconcile this knowledge with the tenets of his religion.

Eleni's marriage had been a good one, her Stavros had grown to maturity with the birth of his first son and she had borne him more children. He had been a good worker, supporting his growing family through good years and bad and the little farmstead had thrived with more sons working alongside him, and daughters too, Christina's brother, Christa, and an older sister, but Stavros had died some years since and left Eleni in her widowhood. She thought back now on those dear memories as she sat there.

She dozed intermittently as the sun moved slowly towards the distant horizon, shining through the vine leaves and making dappled patterns on the flagstones, a gentle breeze blowing off the sea, shifting and stirring them, constantly changing the light and shadow beneath. A low buzzing of insects and the occasional contented clucking of the hens pecking about the yard, the only sound in the quiet of the afternoon. Tiny iridescent lizards scuttled across the ground and scaled the adobe walls and sometime, a great horned beetle came out of a crevice, its carapace glistening enamelled black.

In a while, Christina came out of the farmhouse bringing a long glass of cold, pressed orange juice for her grandmother, setting it down beside her while she crouched on the paving at her feet.

The old lady started awake from her dozing and put her arm around the girl's shoulders. Christina pressed Eleni's hand and leant against her knee.

"I shall have to go away soon, Grandma. They're all beginning to watch me. I can't face them with the truth, but you know it, don't you?"

Eleni nodded, "Yes my dear, but where will you go? Will you go to see Father Antoni? Have you written to him? He's back in the village."

"I know I can't go back to working in his house now, he doesn't know about the baby but Ariadne will soon be having her's and I should stay and help her. Oh Grandma, I love him, I can't ruin his career. What shall I do?"

The two women sat silently together for a long while but then it was time for Christina to go back down to the village to be with Ariadne. She had come up to the farmstead in the early morning with Stavros who had done some woodwork in the house and he was anxious to get home before dark, Ariadne being near her time. He called out to Christina that he was finished with the work and ready to leave, so she got to her feet, kissed Eleni and took the old lady's empty glass back to the house. The family all hugged her, telling her to look after herself – did they mean because of her condition, could they have guessed – and then, laughing and waving, saw her climb into Stavros' rather battered old car laden with fruit and vegetables and gifts for the baby and they set off back down the mountainside bumping over the rough track.

Anthony slipped back quietly and unannounced into the village and made his way to the little curacy house, noting as he stepped through the gate, the new little statuette by the door and the colourfully planted pots at either side. Inside he looked around appreciatively, smiling at the brightly patterned new curtains at the window and the other small touches that Ariadne and Christina had brought into his austere, bachelor surroundings. As he unpacked his few belongings, he turned over in his mind again, the problem of his brief, passionate relationship with Christina. Would she want to return to work in his house, could he ever contemplate employing her again? His retreat in the monastery had given him time to concentrate on the way that his future life would develop and his visit back to Ireland and his large, happy family, had decided him that he was not suited to monastic life; he had more to give to the people of this parish and he would be able to serve them and take over more of Father Georgio's duties, giving the old man more time for his reading.

First he had to report to Father Georgios that he was back to resume his parochial duties and then get himself some food and make his domestic arrangements, the cleaning, cooking and laundering that were necessary, which he knew from Father Giorgio's letters Christina's sister had been managing while Christina had been staying with her family up in the mountains, caring for Eleni.

After washing in the tepid water from the tap over the sink, Anthony changed into his cassock, which he found pressed and hung ready for him and he went out to make his way to the house.

Father Giorgio was, as usual at this hour, prior to evensong, sitting out on his verandah, a glass of wine beside him.

They fell easily into conversation, Father Giorgio wanting to hear all about Anthony's stay at the monastery and of the subsequent visit to Ireland and his large family and how he had spent his time there. The old man was pleased at Anthony's decision to return to parish life rather than choose to enter the enclosed order of the brotherhood, as his friend from their student days had done. He brought Anthony up to date with the happenings in the village, some births, some deaths and various services he had taken to celebrate these. He didn't mention

Christina though. He didn't want to enquire too closely into the situation between her and Anthony as it stood now; he hadn't seen her, though he knew she had been staying with her sister for some time, helping her prepare for her confinement. Anthony too avoided the topic, he needed to sort out things himself, between the two of them.

For now the two priests must make their arrangements for the greatest event in the ecclesiastical calendar – Easter – which would be upon them in a few days. Services had to be planned, altar boys rehearsed in their duties, the women of the parish organised for the cleaning of the great silver Easter candlesticks and sconces and the flower arranging – all would be willing to help with these tasks they knew, but also knew that there could be arguments over who was responsible for which particular duties and resultant bad feelings aroused. Georgios sighed deeply at the prospect, he had encountered it all many times before, and he was glad to have Anthony deputise for him.

The following morning, Anthony was woken by the sounds of activity in the kitchen, the clatter of pans and the clink of china accompanied by the tantalising aroma of freshly ground coffee. He got up quickly and pulled on jeans and a sweater and made his way out there. The table was already set for breakfast, a fresh baked loaf, still warm from the oven sat on a round wooden platter, with butter and a jar of dark honey beside it. There were flowers in a blue pottery jug and a white, checked napkin bedside his plate and, standing at the stove, Christina. She turned towards him, not smiling but tense, with a strained expression. Her long hair was pulled back from her face into a tight knot, her blouse buttoned to her neck, a large sacking apron tied around her waist over a sombre black skirt. She looked – dressed as she was – like one of the older village woman.

She was the first to speak, in a rush she asked if she should make Anthony an omelette or scramble him some eggs, not enquiring as to how he was faring in the long weeks away at the retreat in the monastery or on his visit to his family in Ireland.

Anthony found himself unable to respond, he just nodded his head to her suggestions – he hadn't any appetite for breakfast. He poured himself coffee and cut a thick slice of bread and almost automatically spread it with butter and honey.

Christina moved into the bedroom and fetched the bed clothes to air on the line outside. Anthony watched her; what was she thinking as she stripped the bed where they had lain together at their last meeting? She moved about silently, sweeping and dusting. Anthony wondered how she could act so normally, he knew from his conversation with Father Giorgio that she had been helping her sister who was near the time of her confinement; did Ariadne know of Christina's forbidden involvement with himself?

When Christina came back into the room, still silently, she gathered up his breakfast things and took them to the sink. Anthony followed her with his eyes, wanting to ask her so many things, to apologise to her for breaking all the rules of his calling. He questioned in his mind, as he had so often over the past weeks, what he should do now, now that he was back in the village, questioning still his priesthood while practicing his faith and urging his parishioners to observe their's.

Christina reappeared, her apron removed and folded into her basket, preparing to leave. Now she spoke and explained that after her sister's confinement she would no longer be able to work for Anthony and could recommend a young village girl who would take over from her and would be able to begin working the next day.

Christina would come with her to show her around the house and explain to her what would be required of her. She looked at Anthony, her eyes filling with tears, he stepped towards her, holding out his hand, but she shook her head and hurried out the door.

Christina brushed the tears from her cheek and congratulated herself on keeping her decision not to speak to Anthony of their lovemaking, she didn't want to have his whole career ruined through this one fall from grace – as his superiors would most certainly judge it to have been and she was determined that her resulting pregnancy would remain a secret. Her family too shouldn't learn of it, she would go away and find work elsewhere on the island – she was confused, only her grandmother, Eleni, had guessed the truth and Christina knew that she could trust her implicitly to keep the knowledge to herself. How she was to manage she didn't know but after seeing Ariadne through her confinement, she would leave the village and lose herself until her own time came.

When she reached Ariadne's, she found her sister and Stavros in a great state of excitement, the midwife had been alerted, an old woman from the next village who had seen most of the young people into the world. Stavros was just about to set off in his car to fetch her and Christina immediately set to, to prepare for the imminent delivery, fetching a pan of water to put on the stove to boil as she had observed was required at these events.

Anthony, meanwhile, had gone to Father Giorgio to get his instructions for the tasks to be undertaken for the Easter festival and he was soon in the church getting the special Easter candlesticks and altar cloth from the cupboards in the vestry and overseeing the dusting and polishing of the pews and the pulpit with its great winged eagle and intricate carvings. The villagers brought in sheaves of spring flowers and greenery to decorate this and the grey, stone-slabbed font.

Everywhere there was a happy hubbub, Anthony had little time to think of his brief meeting with Christina at breakfast, she had seemed different, remote, he had noted her drab clothes and the way her hair had been tightly drawn back from her face and pinned into a severe plain coil at her nape. Her face had been pale and pinched but he supposed that she had felt shy with him, as he had felt towards her, though his heart had lurched in his chest at the sight of her.

The next day, she arrived with the young woman who was to take over his housekeeping and he found the opportunity to speak to her while the new incumbent dealt with the bed-making, slipping apologetically between them carrying the linen to hang on the line in the yard to air beneath the catalpa tree and be infused with the scents of the frangipani and the sweet herbs there.

Anthony wanted to apologise for his past actions but Christina waived aside his attempts to do so; he had to insist that she accepted money from him in respect of how she had looked after his house while he was away and payment for the new curtains that had been put up. But it was all a cold and business-like transaction, he barely touched her hand when he put the money into it and she put the folded notes into her purse with a briefly murmured thanks and turned back to showing her successor where to find various items in the kitchen until it was time for them to go.

Ariadne's' baby had been born, a boy, and the christening was planned for a few days after the Easter services, while the church was still decorated with flowers; Anthony was to officiate. He stood at the font, clad in his white vestments and embroidered stole and watched Christina, the child's godmother, take the baby in her arms and cradle it lovingly. Anthony thought she had never looked so beautiful, her hair released from the tight chignon she'd worn at their last encounter, shining in the light of the christening candles surrounding the font. Her dress colourful and low cut so that he saw the baby reach up and catch the little gold crucifix that she wore on a chain around her neck and which she gently took from the infant's tiny fingers.

Anthony could hardly begin speaking the words of the christening service, he was overwhelmed with feelings that he had fought to submerge in his work at the monastery and when he had been with his family in far off Ireland; to see Christina standing there with the baby in the crook of her arm, he had to make an enormous effort and draw a deep breath before he could utter a word.

There was feasting after the christening, Christina's and Ariadne's family and Stavros' too, parents, brothers and sisters. Dear Eleni who had come to see her first great-grandchild received into the church, her lined brown face framed in a black shawl, her clothes all black. Anthony excused himself after greeting them all with a special word for Eleni who now seemed old and frail; she was delighted when she was given the newly christened Lukas to hold and sat crooning to him until Ariadne took him to feed. Christina kept occupied passing round plates of sweetmeats and the tiny glasses of ouzo that Stavros poured for everyone to toast his son, avoiding Anthony's eyes as she passed amongst the guests.

Christina had no difficulty in finding work, it was a busy time on the land and she had plenty of experience helping out on her parents' smallholding. She didn't stay long in one place, she didn't want Anthony, nor anyone else, family or friends from the village, to find her as she made her way further away from them and deeper and higher into the mountainous interior of the island.

No one commented on her pregnancy which was becoming obvious. She was a strong, healthy young woman and a hard worker, long days in the fields brought a glow to her skin and the sun tanned it to a deeper gold and shone on her long, dark hair; many of her fellow labourers sought her out to share their midday packs of bread and cheese and fruit washed down with rough, red wine, sitting beneath the shade of olive and almond trees and the vine rows that lined the hillsides. Many nights she would sleep in the open under the clear, starry Aegean sky, on her way to another farm or room to be made for her, a trestle bed in the corner of some stone-flagged farmhouse kitchen, or on a verandah beneath a canopy of bougainvillea clambering over the wooden beams above her and meals shared with the family, great bowls of fresh pasts with thick slices of home baked bread to rub around the earthenware plates to soak up the rich, garlic flavoured tomato sauces; it was a healthy diet and Christina and her baby thrived on it.

She was, however, beginning to tire more easily and finding it more difficult to move along the vegetable rows, her back aching as she bent to pull up the carrots and radishes and clear the weeds growing amongst them. She began to think lovingly of her home and her family and friends in the village – and Anthony. Her last meeting with him had been so perfunctory, so business-like and he was still not aware of his child that she was carrying. She had long since spent the money that he had given her, but she wore the little gold crucifix all the time, touching it every now and again as it lay against her breast

64

and moved with her as though it was some kind of talisman protecting the baby, his baby.

So, after some five months, Christina began to make her way back across the island, down craggy mountain paths, sometimes given a lift in a donkey cart with her small bundle of clothes and few belongings, or walking for miles along the deep valleys between the lower, vine-clad hills, stopping a day here, a week there, working her way slowly back in the direction of the village.

The sun blazed down on her and her feet ached as she stumbled along the rough pathways, their flints and grit working up through her sandals, her ankles swollen in the heat. She met with many kindnesses, was welcomed into small farmsteads and shared their food in return for working on easier tasks about their holdings, and given lifts in carts along her way.

Sometimes, as she lay tired and aching after another long day working in the open, but not able to get to sleep, Christina pondered restlessly over her situation and her thoughts turned to Anthony, she began to wonder about what had happened between them and question her feelings for him. Was it just the fact of their being brought together by her working for him – was it her fault perhaps that she had allowed herself to think of him as more than her employer? She had looked at his family photographs and he had told her about his parents and brothers and sisters pictured in them and she had been interested, but would she have been so interested in any foreigner's photographs and in learning their strangely spelt and odd sounding names? Of course she had taken pride in her work, housekeeping for the clergy was a coveted job for village girls and she'd provided homely touches, putting flowers on the breakfast table, cooking his favourite meals, bringing him gifts of honey from Eleni's bees but had Anthony ever made any inappropriate advances to her? He had given her a little crucifix and taken the trouble to have it engraved with her name, but wasn't it just a token of his appreciation of her efforts and a proper choice of gift from a priest?

Then there came that last evening when they both had their feelings overcome them, she had felt this was true love and gave herself to him and Anthony had renounced his vows in that moment of passion and given himself to her. Neither of them had considered the consequences. He had gone away to the monastery, on retreat, and had time to think there, amongst those celibate religious men, about what had happened while she was left behind and in a few weeks had found herself to be pregnant with his child. She thought bitterly that it had been harder for her, she hadn't told him about the baby, protecting him and his career, but she was having to bear all the responsibility of her situation.

Christina tossed and turned and felt the baby moving, a fluttering in her belly and put a hand over its swelling to still it.

The pain began suddenly, stabbing at her belly and taking her breath away. She gasped and felt a trickle of warm liquid slide down her thighs; another sharp thrust of pain and she knew the baby was coming. She looked around her desperately, she was on an open plain, it was deserted, no sign of farmsteads or shepherd's huts where she might get shelter and help.

The sun was high in the wide, cloudless, brilliant blue sky, its rays beating down on her, unbearably hot, there was no shade anywhere, no trees nor planted rows of vines, just scrub and scattered outcrops of rocks. The path she was following, narrow and dusty and spiked with flints. She spotted a little hollow in the ground a short distance ahead, set back from the path, with a few boulders around its rim. She left the path and limped across to it, breathless with the pain of her hastening contractions. Feeling like a wounded animal, she lay down, the sun's heat radiated off the rocks and small lizards scuttled into the crevices between them, disturbed by her sudden appearance – the scents of wild thyme and oregano crushed by her weight, rose up around her, her sweat mingling with them.

It was over quite soon, the baby slid from her and she caught its tiny, bloodied body. The cord followed, she had nothing to cut it with and the child lay lifeless against her. She massaged its tiny limbs as she'd seen the shepherds do to their new-born lambs and she tried to breathe life into its puckered lips, but there was no response, born too soon and unaided it lay still in her arms.

Christina, exhausted and frightened, pulled herself upright to sit with her back against one of the rocks. She reached into the bag she'd been carrying with her and extracted a clean shirt from it to wipe the infant free of mucous and blood before wrapping it closely and then pulled out more clothes to clean herself and staunch her own blood flow. She stroked the baby's thin wisps of blond hair, like Anthony's, and on impulse pulled off from around her neck, the crucifix that he had given her and put it in her son's palm, closing the tiny fingers tightly around it and tucking his hand back beneath the swaddling shirt.

Christina laid back down on the tumbled crush of herbs, exhausted and weak, the baby still in the fold of her arm. Her heart beat wildly, her brain in turmoil, what was she to do now? The child dead – Anthony had never known of her pregnancy so he wouldn't mourn his loss, she could leave the baby there in the mountains. No one need ever know of his birth – except Eleni. How she wished the old lady was with her now, with her wisdom and understanding. Would she understand if Christina abandoned the poor, stillborn child? It was all too much to think of yet she must rest. She shifted so that the largest rock at least partly shaded her from the sun, still high in the sky, and easing the baby from her embrace, she laid him a little way from her in the shade of another of the encircling boulders. She remembered the bottle of wine she had carried from her last employment, filled for her journey by the farmer's wife to sustain her on her way, with a crusty loaf of bread and some cheese. She reached once more into her rucksack to get the bottle, it was almost half empty but she took a small draught of it, sweet and warm, she swallowed it, the liquid soothing her dry throat and calming her frantic, racing thoughts. Replacing the cork, she put the bottle carefully back into the bag, arranging her spare clothes around it to protect it from the intense heat, then laid herself down once more.

She soon fell asleep and when she awoke it was dusk and the air had cooled. She knew now what she must do and, selecting a sharp flint from the ground around her, scraped away some of the sun—baked dry earth from where she had rested and very tenderly set down the baby, packing soft foliage from the herbs there, over and around the tiny body and finding a wild cyclamen growing nearby she picked a single flower and laid it above the small mound of soil that covered him. She said a little prayer for her child and then, gathering up her things, made her way back to the path and began her journey homewards again.

She hadn't gone too far before the high walls of the convent where she had attended school came into view, set high above the desolate plain she was travelling through. Tired and bleeding she struggled on with renewed strength of purpose, knowing she could find sanctuary there.

It was nearly dark now, the first stars glittered above her and the rising moon gave some light, helping her pick her way along the rough and winding stony track. The rustling of small animals in the undergrowth accompanied her without frightening her, but she feared the snakes that might be lurking there too and worried that if she tripped and stumbled, and perhaps twisted her ankle, she might lie undiscovered like her baby and the vipers would slither out from their cover and twine around her, sucking at her flesh.

With increasingly frequent pauses to rest and to take small sips of wine from her bottle, she slowly began to gain the upward slopes of the hill ahead of her and climbed purposefully to reach the farmed fields and vineyards that were laid out in geometric formality surrounding the convent. Here were smoother flattened tracks, weaving through the rows that led to the outbuildings, sheds and stables and great storage barns. Christina stopped by one of these and crept under its sheltering eaves to ease her limbs, aching from her ascent and to take off her sandals to shake loose the grit that had worked up between her toes and rubbed at her heels. Then she put them back on and with a final, desperate effort, lifting her bag, she made her way the last few hundred yards into the confines of the main convent building and reaching the great iron gates she pulled the bell rope hanging beside them and collapsed exhausted and faint onto the floor.

The sisters were at evening prayers when they were disturbed by the deep jangle of the bell; did they imagine it; who would be seeking admittance at this hour? Sister Joseph who was the door keeper tonight, excused herself from the service and with a quick obeisance towards the altar, hurried out of the chapel and made her way through the darkening cloister to the entrance hall and the door that led to the high, barred gate outside. She picked up a lantern from an adjacent niche in the plain whitewashed walls and held it high as she unlocked the door and stepped out into the night. Her candle flickering, she walked across the paved courtyard to the gate. Struggling with the huge iron key that she wore hung on a chain over her habit, she turned it in the lock and pulled the heavy, ornate gate inwards. Looking down she saw the huddle of clothes that was Christina, now unconscious. Leaving the gate ajar, Sister Joseph ran back to the chapel; the other nuns were coming out from it, their service over and she called to the Mother Superior to come at once and to the others to bring help.

They almost ran with her, though it was unheard of to move at other than a respectful, slow pace, with downcast eyes and keeping to the inner wall of the high arched passageway. Mother Superior sped to the front of the group and was first to reach Christina and kneel by her, noting her blood-stained clothing and feeling for a pulse. Satisfied that she was still alive, she instructed two of the sisters to lift and carry her into the convent; another brought her rucksack and the heavy gate was swung closed and locked again by Sister Joseph, who followed the other women into the house.

Christina was laid gently onto the couch in the visitor's room; one of the sisters brought a jug of water and sponged her face, while another was despatched to make up a bed in the infirmary across the cloistered atrium. Christina lay prone, her eyes closed, her breathing slow and faint.

Christina slept all the next day, the nuns taking it in turns to sit by her bed, ready to report when there was any change in her. When she finally awoke, it took her some time to realise where she was and how she had got there. She now lay between crisp, white sheets, washed and dressed in a long white gown, her hair combed and spread around her head on the pillows. The young nun beside her, seeing her open her eyes, bent over her smiling sweetly and putting an arm around her shoulders to raise up her head, held a glass of water to Christina's dry lips. Christina swallowed a little of it gratefully and slipped back onto her pillow. The nun, smiling reassuringly, left her and went to tell the Mother Superior that their guest had awakened.

Instructions were given for some hot soup to be prepared and brought for the patient and then the older nun started across to the infirmary. The sisters responsible for nursing and tending the occupants of the few, white painted, iron bedsteads that were laid out in two rows either side of the sunlit ward, met with her at the doorway and confided their findings. It appeared that this unfortunate young woman had very recently given birth and that from the state of her feet, had walked many miles, so scratched, blistered and swollen were they.

Mother Superior approached Christina's bed. There were only two others occupied, one by a very elderly, dozing nun who had been confined to the infirmary for some long time as she had become too frail to continue in the daily routines of prayer and study and the heavy work about the house and on the land that supplied most of the food for the convent. In the other bed, a young novice was recovering from a bout of fever; she was sitting up and reading her missal and bowed her head to the visitor in respectful, silent greeting.

Christina went to sit up as Mother Superior came to her bedside but the nun motioned her to remain as she was and drawing up a heavy wooden chair, sat down by her.

Conversation was restrained and not interrogatory. No mention was made concerning the findings of the nurses, only remarking how far Christina must have walked to have so hurt her feet, to which Christina merely nodded her agreement.

A bowl of steaming broth was soon brought and Mother Superior assisted Christina to sit upright and arranged her pillows to support her and with an injunction to take the soup while it was hot, Mother Superior left the ward with a nod and a kindly smile to the novice.

Christina spent the next few days hovering between sleep and wakefulness. Asleep her mind was troubled with dark dreams from which she awoke frightened and disorientated, her sheets damp with sweat, tangled about her limbs. Then one of the nuns would tend to her, changing her gown and bed linen and encouraging her to take milk or soup. The herbalist sister prepared poultices and ointments from her store of healing herbs that grew in her plot in the convent garden, to treat her scarred and swollen feet and mixed herbal infusions from age-old recipes for her to drink.

The young novice was allowed to get out of her bed now, for a few hours each day and after she had washed and dressed she tidied her pristine sheets and coverlet – no doubt involuntarily regretting that she would soon have to revert to sleeping on the hard, narrow, wooden bed that awaited her in her cell, on the thin, horsehair stuffed mattress and single flat pillow, encased in its coarse cotton cover, with only a roughly woven blanket over her that scratched uncomfortably against her skin. She went across to where Christina lay and smoothed her hot sheets and turned her pillows so that their linen covers were cool against her cheek and then she refreshed the water in the stoneware jug that stood with a thick green glass tumbler on the plain wooden locker by the bed, alongside a Bible and a small carved crucifix; then she lifted Christina's head and helped her to drink a little, stroking her hair back from her burning forehead.

Outside the sun was blazing down, silhouetting the branches and leaves of the tall trees surrounding the building against the long white curtains at the infirmary windows and dappling their patterns onto the cool tiled floor. The thick stone walls of the building withstood the intense heat and kept it cool within.

When she was awake, Christina could see out of the nearest windows opposite her bed and observe small birds fluttering about outside, pecking at the leaves and berries, and could watch the evening sky turn burnished copper in the treeless, barren valley floor which figured so often in her dreams and prayers.

Gradually her strength returned and Christina was able to take a few steps about her bed, holding onto the rail end and flexing the new-formed skin on her toes and blistered heels against the soothing coolness of the floor tiles. Day by day she progresses a little further and Mother Superior came to visit her again.

She had not been in charge when Christina had attended the convent school so had no way of recognising her from those early days but in their conversation she realised that Christina knew the area around the convent and that she had worked on the small farms and vineyards beyond and possibly had family in the mountains. The nun made no reference to the circumstances that had brought the young woman to the convent seeking shelter, only expressing her satisfaction that the sisters' devoted nursing was showing progress in Christina's physical condition and her belief that she would soon be strong enough to make plans for her future – a future that Christina had not yet felt able to contemplate.

As she lay there listening to the quiet activities of the convent, the gentle regular tolling of the chapel bell calling the nuns to their devotions, the patter of their sandaled feet hurrying through the cloisters and their murmured conversations, she felt comfort in these sounds and she smelt the scents of fresh mown hay and the heady aroma of wild flowers and herbs wafting through the narrow opening of the tall infirmary windows and nearer, the smells of cooking accompanied by the occasional clatter of pots and pans from the kitchen, all of which tempted her returning appetite for the simple healthy and sustaining food being prepared there. Christina knew she had decisions to make.

Now that they were both recovering, Christina was having long conversations with Sophia, the young novice. Christina was interested to learn how the girl had come to the convent; what had decided her to give up so much, in Christina's view, her family and friends, the prospects of love and marriage and children of her own in the future. Sophia met all Christina's queries with a calm and gently smiling response.

She was one of a huge family, she explained, who owned land and property on the island. She had had a privileged upbringing, being educated in a convent school and had done well in her studies. A great future had been envisaged for her, possibly in the law or teaching but Sophia had felt from an early age the attraction of the religious life. She had admired the nuns who taught her and envied their simple lifestyle, the regular pattern of their days, punctuated by calls to prayer and their serenity and very apparent happiness in their calling. As a novice, she had come to take part in the convent's daily routines, she enjoyed the hard physical work in the garden; in the bustling steamy laundry with the chatter and laughter of the sisters as they folded and fed their linen through the rollers of the great iron mangle, and in the kitchen where as a novice she scrubbed and polished the black iron pots and copper pans. All far removed from what she had known in her previous life before she entered the Convent. Always a serious student, she also looked forward to advancing her religious knowledge when she made her final vows and would be allowed to study in the Convent library and have access to the Holy Scriptures and religious writings stored there in great leather-bound books and illuminated manuscripts handed down through the Order over many years, testament to the sisters' patient and ordered penmanship and gilding skills.

Sophia announced how free she felt now, in this place, protected from the harsh realities of life in the world outside the convent walls. She knew the peasants in the mountains and the local villagers in their small communities had to work very hard to get a living and often had worries as to where their next meal would come from if their domestic animals fell ill, their few chickens laid no eggs or their crops failed due to drought, burnt too dry in the rock-hard earth by the constant blazing sunshine. She didn't ask Christina about her situation but Christina volunteered to tell a little of her life, in their school which served the few scattered villages down beyond the Convent's mountain eyrie, how she too had been taught by these same nuns whose hospitality and care she was now receiving, until she was fourteen and left to work with her family on their mountain farmstead. Christina was quite recovered physically now from the ordeal of her lonely labour in childbirth, but the trauma of her conscience at her hiding the baby in the scrubby undergrowth of the barren, rocky valley down beyond the convent and the long, hard, footsore stumbling walk to achieve its sheltering walls, remained with her.

She knew that she would have to make her confession and the thought scared her although she could rely on her confidentiality being totally respected, the mere fact of putting into words the sequence of events that would bring her finally to seek absolution, was terrifying. She felt that she was quite alone in her predicament and that she had no one she could turn to who would understand the enormity of her dual crimes; having illicit relations with her priest and her abandonment of their child, albeit the baby had been stillborn: even Anthony, if he were to learn of her actions, could he ever forgive her?

But for the present, Christina decided to seek an interview with the Mother Superior and request that she could stay at the Convent awhile and work – perhaps as a lay sister, to repay in part the care she had received from the nuns, to give her more time to review her situation and make plans for the future.

She considered whether she should go further and enter the novitiate, with the prospect that that would give of her taking the final vows and retreating permanently behind the Convent walls. She recalled that some of her classmates at school had done so, though they had stayed as students longer than her and had more time to consider fully the consequences and in a more adult way than perhaps based on an adolescent crush on a particular teacher as often occurred in Catholic schools. Teachers and nurses did go out from the Order but their lives were fairly restricted and they always had to return to the mother house, marriage and children of their own denied them by their vow of celibacy.

Her heart ached for Anthony. She could recall every nuance of their intimacy when they were both inevitably overpowered by their feeling for each other; the warmth of his body as he had lain beside her, the scent of him, their abandonment of every thought other than the fulfilment of the passion that overcame them – and their last meeting, so restrained and perfunctory, he knowing only of his lapse of faith and neither of them yet of the child they had begun to create.

Chapter Eight

Ariadne, Stavros and little Lukas were very settled and happy in Eleni's old cottage. Stavros had plenty of work and Ariadne was contented looking after their home, feeding the chickens and tending their small vegetable plot and enjoying baby Lukas who was growing rapidly. The days went by quickly; she sometimes took Lukas down to the beach and watched him happily discovering the small creatures in the rock pools and making determined efforts to venture further, crawling rapidly across the sand to the water's edge where he chortled delightedly as the waves rolled towards him and slid gently over his hands and knees and Ariadne raced to gather him up, dangling him in the water while he kicked at each approach of breaking surf.

They had no news of Christina, nor had any of her family. Anthony, sometimes when he saw them in church or called on them in the course of his pastoral rounds and occasionally stayed to share a meal with them, would enquire if they had any news of her but only in a general way, it would seem, as he would of any of his parishioners. He was well satisfied with the work of Christina's successor in caring for his house and didn't admit to missing Christina's special little touches – the fresh posies of flowers on his breakfast table or the sprigs of fragrant herbs folded into his carefully laundered clothes.

Only very occasionally did Ariadne and Stavros make the trip into the mountains to visit the family farmstead and neither was there any news of Christina known there.

Eleni had now become very frail and was unable to help with the work outside and only a little with cooking indoors, mostly she would sit out under the shade of the vine covered pergola, dozing. She delighted in Ariadne's visits with Lukas, happy to hold the baby on her lap, cooing to him and kissing him, the little boy responding to her with cheerful gurgling, gripping her old bent fingers and pulling at strands of the long, white hair escaping from beneath her black headscarf; Eleni wondered would she soon have another great-grandchild to hold.

The old nun who had lain in bed in the infirmary while Christina was convalescing there, had now become increasingly weak and could not be expected to live much longer. Mother Superior had decided it was time to send for the priest to administer to the aged sister. She had known her a long time, since indeed she had come under her care soon after completing her novitiate and she had the greatest respect for her and her wide-ranging religious knowledge. She visited the old lady every day, finding time within her heavy schedule to sit with her, talking or reading to her. Now she asked if she would like the priest to come and felt the gentle pressure of her old fingers in her own hand.

Christina was now working in the convent and she was on duty in the infirmary, attending to counting the bed linen and sorting it on the wide shelves in the laundry room at the far end of the ward, when the priest arrived with Mother Superior and an attendant nursing sister. Christina couldn't leave the ward while they were approaching down its length so she waited where she was in the little white painted, windowless cell and watched.

The priest's head was bent and turned towards Mother Superior who walked beside him, so Christina couldn't see his face, but a shaft of sunlight through one of the long windows in the ward, fell on his head and his blond hair gleamed and as he drew near, he raised his head and Christina's heart lurched and she nearly gasped aloud as she recognised the young man. Their eyes met, he looked at her frowning in puzzled recognition. Christina stepped back further into the shadow of the laundry room.

While Mother Superior and the nun busied themselves putting screens around the bed, Christina seized the opportunity and fled, almost running, her sandals slapping noisily on the tiled floor. Mother Superior glared over her shoulder at the retreating figure, resolving to admonish the girl for disturbing the silence of the ward in her hasty retreat.

Christina continued to hurry along the wide, stone corridors and out into the open. Keeping close to the wall, she made her way to the dormitory house where the lay women workers were accommodated. She burst through the outer door and reached the long, dark room where her bed was positioned halfway down its length and sat down upon it trembling, her heart pounding so that it felt as though it would break out of her breast. Had he recognised her? He had seemed to look directly at her – he wouldn't, couldn't, have expected to find her here in the convent. Christina's mind was in turmoil, what was she to do? She sat where she was a long time, struggling with her thoughts.

Anthony had not expected to officiate at the old nun's funeral which took place a few days later, she having died peacefully in her sleep. Father Giorgio usually dealt with matters requiring a priest's attendance at the Convent but he was getting older and deputed a good deal of pastoral work to the younger priest. The nun, having no family, the burial was to take place in the grounds amid several others where there had been no relatives to take the body from the convent. Their last resting place was a peaceful, secluded area, high on the mountain side, beautifully tended gardens surrounding their graves, marked with plain granite crosses. Birds sang in the branches of the sheltering trees and the views all round stretched for miles. Most of the nuns followed and some of the lay workers. Christina stayed on the edge of the group that

79

crowded around the young priest. She had come for she wanted to see Anthony, she had yearned for him for months past and now she could get near him but could she get close as they had to each other in their forbidden relationship?. She had come to a decision eventually and comforted herself that it would be possible for her to make her confession to him as the nuns regularly made theirs to the priests and she could tell him of the child they had made together; she could make a clean breast of her guilty action in abandoning the still-born infant and face whatever his reaction, perform her formal penance and receive absolution.

The newly risen sun was beginning to warm the air which was fragrant with the scent of herbs and wild flowers, the last blossoms fluttered onto the ground blown by a gentle breeze. As the final spadeful of earth was smoothed over the disturbed ground and the simple cross placed at its head, the nuns repeated their prayers and sang a hymn, then moved closer with the lilies they carried to decorate the grave. Then the group made their way back to the main house and through the cloisters to the chapel. The nuns entered it quietly and prayed together again for the soul of their dear departed sister.

Christina now had firmly resolved that she would ask Mother Superior if she might make confession when the priest next came to the convent to hear the nuns'.

Anthony gave a brief blessing in the chapel and went out with the Mother Superior to her private study to take some refreshment before he journeyed back down into the village, He rode a Lambretta to get up and down the steep hill on which the convent was perched and his departure was a noisy one as he sped off, his stole folded and soutane tucked up beneath him, the tools of his office secured in a box behind him on the carrier rack.

Christina couldn't approach him then but she sought out Mother Superior at the earliest opportunity and made her request. It was not unusual for lay helpers to make their confessions in the convent and the nun who wanted to assist this young woman to find the peace of mind that obviously eluded her and help her resolve the problems that had led her to find sanctuary here in the convent, readily agreed that Christina should make her confession at the priest's next visit for that purpose.

In a few weeks' time, Anthony came to the convent again to hear the nuns' confessions. Christina thought they could not have very much to confess, perhaps some outburst of irritation at one of the other sisters or maybe forgetting to put salt in the big, black iron pan of tomatoes that were boiled up every day for the pasta sauce to be served in the refectory for their evening meal, what possible sins could these holy women commit in their enclosed contemplative environment? Yet how soothing to feel that in confiding their very minor misdemeanours to their confessor and repeating the hail Mary's and prayers ordered by him, all would be forgiven, the slate wiped clean and their lives could go in in renewed spiritual devotion. How sheltered they were from the ordinary problems of the lives led by the people outside the convent walls; even if they were among those who did go out in the community, nursing or teaching and exposed to the everyday trials of the local artisans and farmers, they came back into the peace and security of the great stone building on the hill and the regimented, austere way of life, lived by the ancient rules laid down by the early saints.

When the nuns had taken their turns in the small, closed panelled closet of the confessional in the side aisle of the chapel, Christina was called from her work and made her way anxiously there. She was shaking as she fumbled with the brass handle and opened the door. She stepped inside and shut it behind her.

It was dark in the interior and it took some minutes to accustom her eyes to the shadows. She sat down on the narrow wooden bench and looked up at the grille behind which she knew Anthony was waiting.

She didn't know how to begin and his voice came to her, speaking the well-known form of words he had repeated so many times in his work, designed to put the penitent at ease and assure total confidentiality.

Her heart was beating so hard in her breast, Christina thought Anthony would surely be able to hear it thudding as she struggled to speak her responses and begin to find the words to confess her sin and her deep regret for what she had done. When she described the birth of the child and how she had tried in vain to breathe life into him and continued to describe his burial, there was a choking sound, a sob? And Anthony's hand appeared at the grille between them. He was pushing something through a space in the elaborate iron fretwork, something that gleamed in the shadowy closet and as Christina stretched out her hand towards it, it dropped into her palm, a little gold crucifix on a fine broken chain. She gasped and turned it over and could make out, even in the gloom, her name engraved on the back of it.

How could it have got into his possession? It must mean the baby had been found for she had put the crucifix into its tiny hand as some kind of charm to go with the infant into the unknown world beyond this life, before she covered the little body. How long had Anthony carried it with him – what had happened to the child, indisputably their child, since the cross was found on it? So much to be explained.

Now Anthony was at the confessional door and opening it, he drew Christina out and into his arms, embracing her tenderly and begging her forgiveness for what had happened between them.

Footsteps sounded approaching the main aisle and Christina and Anthony drew quickly apart, each of them realising the impropriety of their position in the surrounding hallowed walls of the convent chapel. Christina still held her crucifix and she hastily put it into the pocket of her apron. Anthony was first to speak, he urgently suggested that he and Christina should meet outside, somewhere away from the convent. She hesitated and he understood that she wouldn't want to go down to the village where she would be recognised and asked where she had been over the past months and possibly even suspected by some of the village elders, gathered in groups in corners, shaking their heads and counting the number of months that she had been away, of having an illicit pregnancy. Anthony walked with her out of the chapel into the cloisters and together they trod the length of the cool, pillared grey stone corridor and out into the sunlit garden. Anthony pulled of his surplice and stole and folded them over his arm as they walked. He guided Christina to a stone bench set beneath the shade of a great catalpa tree facing out toward the rugged mountains beyond, through which Christina had so recently made her lonely way over the many weeks of her homeward journey.

Anthony spread his discarded vestments over the hard stone seat and Christina sat down heavily, staring not at Anthony but to the distant view, afraid to look into his eyes. They sat in silence, around them a gentle breeze stirred the flowers and herbs, releasing their heady scents, bees hummed amongst them and above in the widest, bluest sky, birds dipped and rose again, calling and trilling their various notes.

Anthony began telling her how he had missed her and her daily presence in his home, no one else, he assured her, could ever take her place, he had fallen in love and admitted he had behaved despicably and without any thought for the consequences; had he only known of her pregnancy – which he hadn't even guessed at – he would have done everything to support her. At this Christina turned on him. How could he have done so, his church would surely have called for him to resign his office at once, his career would be finished, where would it all end? There was no child as evidence of what they had done

– as she said this, Christina broke down and wept, recalling again how she had laid the tiny infant in the ground, tucking soft herbs around its fragile limbs before mounding earth over the spot and laying a single, deep pink, cyclamen flower on the top of it – but Anthony must have seen the child, held him and prised the crucifix from the clasp of the small, curled fingers.

It was Anthony's turn to speak. He told Christina how he had been paying a pastoral visit in a nearby village and as he had rested on the cliffside above a small cove on the shore beneath, a young peasant girl had brought a baby to him, she had come across the disturbed earth of the infant's shallow grave and had washed his little body in the sea, before climbing up the path from the shore and seeing Anthony in his clerical garb, had taken the infant to him. He described the feelings that had overwhelmed him when the girl brought Christina's crucifix from her skirt pocket and he realised that the child must be his and he was truly a father not simply as so named by the Catholic Church.

Christina wiped her eyes and look questioningly at Anthony, she couldn't find the words, but he instinctively knew that she wanted to learn from him how he had dealt with the enormous problem facing him as he stood there at the top of the cliff path, holding his dead baby son.

Their conversation was interrupted by a young novice who announced that she had been sent by Mother Superior to find Anthony and advise him there was refreshment awaiting him in her office. He rose to his feet apologetically and Christina stood up too so that he could retrieve his vestments from the bench. He looked from one young woman to the other, hesitating, but Christina excused herself and hurried away without speaking. Anthony looked after her and then followed the nun back into the convent.

Chapter Nine

Back in the village, Anthony completed his day's list of parochial visits as if in a dream. Taking communion to the aged and frailest of his congregation who were unable to make their way to the church; supporting young mothers' tied to their homes with caring for children. His mind was in a turmoil after his meeting with Christina in the Convent and its interruption by the nun reminding him of his invitation to take refreshment with Mother Superior. He had watched Christina walk away without a backward glance, wanting to run after her but as the nun waited for him, unable to do so.

He had accepted the fare laid for him on a crisp, white linen cloth, convent made bread and fine cheese served on the beautifully crafted old pewter platters reserved for important visitors and cool wine in an exquisite glass, he barely tasted any of it, engaging the while in general conversation with his hostess without any sense of its content and with no memory of it after he had left her to make his way back down the mountainside.

Mother Superior had sensed his troubled mind and had wanted to help the young man, to act as his confessor but realising that it might have been the weight of listening to the confessions of her nuns and those of the lay worker, Christina, that preyed on him. Had the girl been able to express to him the circumstances that had brought her to the convent in such distress? Without knowing these herself, she could only pray for them both.

Christina meanwhile, sat alone on her bed in the long, quiet dormitory, fingering the little crucifix in her pocket, numb and exhausted, unable to weep, feeling still the embrace in the chapel with Anthony's arms so briefly, comfortingly around her.

Anthony's last visit of the day was a purely social one, to Ariadne. He wondered if he should tell her that her sister was working in the convent. He knew that the family had no knowledge of her whereabouts and that they were concerned for her.

Ariadne was working in her small garden when Anthony pushed open the wicker gate. Lukas sat on the ground beside her, watching her and reaching out to touch the chickens that strutted and pecked around him, and mimicking their cheeping. He was a delightful happy little boy. Anthony bent to speak to him, his heart aching as he wondered how his own child might have been at this same age, had he lived, and Lukas stretched out his arms to him, wanting to be picked up. Ariadne sat back on her heels and wiped her hands on her pinafore before standing up to welcome Anthony, still carrying Lukas and the three of them moved into the shade at the side of the house and sat down together on the bench there that Stavros had made.

They chatted happily for a while, sharing the friendly gossip of the village. Anthony loosened the collar on his soutane and let Lukas play with his crucifix. He had to stop the little boy from putting it in his mouth in an effort to chew on it. Ariadne laughed and explained he was cutting his teeth and gave him an old, dented wooden rattle to chew on.

Anthony was so enjoying his time with them and shortly Ariadne suggested they go indoors and she'd make them a cool drink. Anthony followed her into the little whitewashed house, still carrying Lukas. He set the child down on the floor with his toys and looked around him. He noted the colourful curtains at the tiny windows, recognising the same gaily patterned fabric as those in his own house that Ariadne had put up for him while he was away and Christina was with her family in the mountains. He ran his hand over the beautifully carved back of his chair, Stavros' work, more of which was evident in the simple furnishings. Brightly woven cushions and mats and pieces of local pottery completed the welcoming effect, a stone jar of wild flowers on a shelf, a terracotta bowl of fruit on the table where Ariadne was setting out a plate of small cakes and a thick glass jug of fresh pressed orange juice and two tall, green glass tumblers.

Anthony was wondering if he should tell her that he had seen Christina; their meeting in the Convent was in the confessional, at least, strictly confidential, the stillborn child – his and hers – a secret, but Ariadne would surely want to know the whereabouts of her sister whom she'd not seen or heard from for so long. He had gone over and over in his mind what he should do ever since he had left the Convent that day, tormented by having to make so many decisions, about Christina, about their child, about his own future. Seeing her again, holding her in the chapel, he had experienced the same feeling for her overwhelming him and his inability to ignore it. He loved her that he was sure of, but had his love to be denied because of his calling?

Looking around him, everything was calm and comfortable by contrast with the austere interior of his clergy house, the contented gurgling and chortles of the little boy, who greedily accepted Anthony's share of cake, after Ariadne had nodded her permission. He realised that it was the presence of mother and child that made this small house truly a home and when Stavros arrived in time to join them and Ariadne fetched another glass, the picture was complete.

The moment was gone when Anthony might have told Ariadne about her sister, he felt that he couldn't burden Stavros with the news of her being at the convent, it would have to wait

87

until another opportunity offered itself. So he drank his orange juice and, refusing another cake, prepared to leave, fastening the collar of his soutane, he bent to ruffle Lukas' curly head then shaking hands with Stavros and Ariadne, he left the little family and turned towards his own lonely home, made the more so by contrast with theirs.

Chapter Ten

Everyone knew by sight the stranger in their midst, they couldn't tell when or exactly how he had come there but he had made a home for himself in an abandoned fisherman's hut at the back of the beach, the roof was sound and the tough wooden shutters could still be closed across the broken window, keeping the blustery on-shore winds at bay. He cooked for himself on driftwood fires laid in the old rusted grate, collecting his fuel – bleached branches and floating flotsam – on his almost daily walks along the strand. He improvised lines from the discarded tackle in the hut and caught fish, grilling them with samphire pulled from amongst the rocks.

They would watch him as he made his way from the old, tarred boarded hut, striding out purposefully. They knew him only as Tony, he hadn't chosen to divulge his full name. Sometimes he would kick a ball that came across his path from the boot of some youngster playing football with a raggle-taggle group of friends and send it curving back to them.

Occasionally he would take time to show the youngsters a scrolled ammonite, etched into the rock and explain its presence there, or teach them how to identify the tiny aquatic creatures living at the water's edge. The children all liked him and gathered around eagerly, sharing their crumpled bags of sticky sweets with him.

In time, winter had come with storms and lightning, the sea grew wilder, breaking in great cascades of water, higher and higher up the beach, threatening to engulf the battered old hut;

so its isolated tenant gave it up and moved into the village, taking up lodging with an elderly widow there.

The locals had become accustomed to seeing him wandering along the strand, this quiet, shy man. That he had lived abroad for some years they had guessed, his deeply tanned skin was evidence of this but they knew nothing of his previous life. Now he began to work intermittently with various village projects, helping to run youth clubs where his athleticism encouraged the youngsters to take part in organised sport. They never questioned his background or qualifications. His lodging was situated on the outskirts of the village, his landlady saw to his needs, cooking his meals and attending to his laundry. She respected his privacy, happy to receive his small regular rent and grateful for his assistance with small household repairs, helping to carry heavy loads of her shopping or putting out rubbish in the yard behind the little terrace house.

She knew that her lodger had family in Dublin – there were some photographs displayed on top of the old-fashioned chest of drawers in his room which she'd noticed when she was cleaning there, but he never mentioned them and only very rarely he visited the city. There was one photo that particularly caught her eye, that of a young woman, darker skinned than the rest, with intense black eyes staring out from the frame, her head thrown back laughing, long dark hair falling about her shoulders and a little crucifix on a chain round her neck. She guessed that this had been someone special in his life but he never mentioned her, the landlady surmising that this girl was someone from the years Tony had spent abroad, her colouring seemed to imply that and she wondered if they'd had some sort of romantic relationship and how it apparently ended.

No one seemed to visit him in his isolated beach hut, the proprietor of the village store and post office reported that sometimes, though very rarely, a letter would come for him addressed to a box number, from overseas, Greece she thought but otherwise he seemed alone without connections of any sort. But his privacy was respected, though in this country where neighbourliness and conviviality was strong - Saturday night ceilidh throughout the year and everyday craic over a pint in the one small pub, his identity was intriguing and the subject of many suggested interpretations and wild imagining.

Anthony had spent long hours going over in his mind how he had acted since his son had been put in his arms, when his whole world had been turned upside down. He had reassured the young peasant girl who had found the baby and so carefully washed the little body in sea water and handed him over, wrapped in a dusty shirt – the only grave clothes that Christina had to cover the child in the ground – that he, Father Anthoni would make all the necessary enquiries as to the circumstances that had led to her discovery and trace the owner of the engraved crucifix that had been clasped tightly in the baby's tiny fingers. He had told her not to speak of her find to avoid any hurtful gossip and that he would arrange for proper burial in consecrated ground and he asked her to pray with him for this abandoned child and for the mother who had suffered such a loss. Then he had given the girl some money and she had gone on her way, rather bewildered but relieved that she had done the right thing in giving the child to the priest that she had been so fortunate to find at the cliff top when she had come up from the beach beneath.

Anthony sat a long time with the baby, covering it with a fold of his soutane. He put Christina's crucifix in his pocket, hoping that maybe he would sometime have the opportunity to return it to her. As dusk fell he moved from the shelter of the wind-sculpted, scraggy trees on the cliff and began to make his way back to the village and into the arid, sparsely inhabited mountains beyond. He walked with no definite direction in mind, just putting one foot in front of the other, stumbling occasionally on a half-buried rock and gripping his bundle more tightly to him.

He followed a narrow track which wound its way upward through the encroaching scrub, flattened by the passage of mule carts and pannier laden donkeys, until he came upon a little wayside shrine at the side of the path. He noted that it was dedicated to Saint Antoni, his own patron saint; its paintwork was faded, the carving around the candle sconce crumbling, the lettering of the saint's insignia hard to make out against the pitted background. Anthony lowered his burden to the ground. Wild thyme and oregano flowered at the base of the shrine, scenting the air about it; this would be a proper place to leave his baby son, the ground consecrated by the siting of the shrine. Anthony knelt awhile and prayed then rose up and looked around him for something with which to dig a grave. He found a few rocks but they weren't suitable, too rounded and heavy then he spotted a large flint – he smashed this down on one of the other boulders and it split as he'd intended it should, to give him the sharp cutting edge that he needed for his sad task.

He cleared away the undergrowth from a small patch behind the shrine and began to cut away the coarse turf beneath. He worked doggedly, scraping off the surface of the ground and gradually digging deeper; this grave must be safe from inquisitive wild animals and passing farmers bringing their produce down to the village below. It was late when Anthony finished his excavation and his only light now was the moon. The night sky was clear and pinpricked with stars, he could see well enough to finish his task. He wrapped the baby more closely then kissed its forehead making the sign of the cross upon it, now he pulled the shirt up over its face and laid the tiny corpse into the bottom of the hole he had dug for it. As he replaced the soil, Anthony repeated the funeral rites in a murmur, praying for the unbaptised child's soul and its safe delivery to the afterlife. He pulled the herbs and wild flowers back over and around the spot and got up from his knees, satisfied that he'd left no sign of disturbance.

Anthony felt exhausted, he had taken the biggest decision of his life, burying the child, but he also felt that he had made the right one for Christina; one day, surely, he would be able to tell her what he had done and they would be able to go together to the little wayside shrine and leave flowers there for their son without anyone but themselves knowing of his existence.

The tall, solitary stranger walked along the beach, the wind blowing his fading, greying blond hair in straggling wisps about his face. He walked barefoot, sometime wading into the waves breaking at the edge of the beach, dipping down occasionally to inspect a rock or pull at a tangled weed, uncovering the small creatures hiding there. Sometimes he would search for a flat-sided pebble and, finding a suitable one, throwing it expertly with a bent arm and watching it bounce, once, twice, three times – and even more – letting out a wild whoop of childish joy at his achievement if the number of the pebbles' bouncing trajectory reached a greater number.

The water was cold, the ripples flecked with oily spume as they broke and receded over the wave-ridged sand. He carried his shoes, the laces tied together, slung around his neck: reaching the far end of the beach where the cliffs rose up and the ground below them was studded with fallen rocks, the man made his way from the sandy shoreline painfully over the pebbles higher up the beach towards these and finding a large, flat-surfaced one, sat down on it and spread out his feet to dry them, picking the gritty sand from between his toes and finally dusting them with his handkerchief which he pulled from a pocket in his rough, worn anorak. A pair of woollen socks tumbled out with the handkerchief and the man retrieved them and began to pull them on. He appeared to struggle for a while to undo the joined laces of his shoes when he took them from around his neck but he finally got them on and unrolled the bottom of his trouser legs. Then he sat for a long time staring out to the distant hazy horizon. What did he see there, a further shore, sunnier maybe? His face was tanned and weather beaten, his blue eyes crinkled against the light reflecting off the water in the pale, elusive northern sunshine.

Chapter Eleven

Eleni was failing fast, she had become increasingly frail for some months now, unable to help around the farm as she had done and with her failing eyesight was not even able to do her lace making, the colourful bobbins falling from her bent, arthritic fingers and tangling the fine threads that ran from them. She stayed in her bed in the shade for most of the day, taking very little food or drink and feeling sadly that she had become a burden to the family; it soon became apparent that she was very near death and word was sent to Ariadne. She and Stavros had visited the old lady once or twice with little Lukas so she wasn't surprised to have this news. Anthony had finally decided to advise her, in strict confidence, of Christina's presence in the convent and now she decided to contact her there. Christina had been a favourite of her grandmother and Ariadne knew they would both want to meet for this one last time, so she asked Stavros to stop at the convent on their way up to the farm and she would persuade Christina to travel with them.

Drawing up at the great iron gates of the convent was awe inspiring. Leaving Stavros in the truck, Ariadne approached the portal and tugged at the rope of the great bell that hung there. Its clangour sounded through the convent and echoed outside the enclosing walls.

Soon, a small shutter in one of the great oaken doors slid aside and a nun's face appeared, smiling behind a wrought metal grille that was now revealed. Ariadne stated her mission. The nun retreated for a few minutes, Ariadne waited as she had been asked to do and then the door was pulled open and she was beckoned inside.

She followed another nun down a long, whitewashed corridor, the floor tiles cool beneath her feet though the day was warm. Everywhere was silent. Ariadne was conscious of the tapping of her shoes following the nun who progressed soundlessly in sandaled feet – only a faint murmur of voices came from the chapel as they passed it and moved on to the refectory and the kitchens.

Ariadne spotted Christina as they went into the great kitchen, she noted that her sister was wearing a coarse brown habit beneath a clean white apron and her hair was drawn back and held by a white kerchief – not quite a nun's veil.

Christina turned from the scrubbed wooden table where she was preparing the vegetable, recognising Ariadne with a frown, but she had no time to ask her how she had known where to find her before Ariadne explained her sad errand.

Christina was shocked to learn of Eleni's feared imminent death and agreed that she should go with Ariadne and Stavros but first, she explained, she would have to ask permission to leave her work. Asking the nun who had brought her to take Ariadne to the visitor's waiting room, Christina took off her apron and went in search of a nun who could sanction her leaving the convent to go with her sister to Eleni. The mistress of novices was quick to take in the obvious shock and pain of Christina's situation and agreed immediately to allow her to leave to visit her grandmother, so in a very short while, Christina joined Ariadne, still attired in the brown habit but with her hair loosed from the white headscarf and they went out together to the waiting truck.

They journeyed almost in silence, Stavros, after greeting Christina, concentrated on his driving over the increasingly uneven and rutted road. As the truck climbed upward, scaling one mountain ridge after another, the track was almost lost sight of as the scrubby undergrowth encroached upon it – and then it would dive down into a greener valley on the sides of which small olive groves were planted in contrasting grey-green foliaged rows and almond trees had shed their leaves onto cultivated plots of vegetation surrounded by retaining dry stone walls built from the larger rocks the strewed the hard, dry earth.

Ariadne was longing to ask Christina about her living at the convent and wondered why she wore that drab nun's habit; had she decided to become a nun herself, it seemed so far from her sister's happy, carefree way of life before she had disappeared so suddenly from the village. She knew that at first Christina had gone to the family smallholding to help with the farm work and assist in Eleni's care but she hadn't stayed there and no one knew where she had gone. Only Anthony, the young priest that Christina had kept house for seemed to be aware of her presence in the convent. He had, she knew, been fond of Christina and her sister had shown Ariadne the little engraved crucifix he had given her at Christmas, but she had thought nothing of this, it was quite a suitable gift from a priest and Christina had been proud to wear it.

Now the road levelled out and the old, stone-built farmstead came into view. A dog ran from it, barking, leaping up as Stavros steered the truck up to the vine-clad patio and parked alongside. The two women got out and were enveloped in their mother's embrace, she looked old and careworn, the farm work was hard and on top of it she had to look after the old woman inside. They all went indoors and the travellers gladly accepted glasses of wine from the cool stone store at the rear of the house before Christina and Ariadne went through to Eleni's room.

The old lady was lying stretched out on her back in the narrow bed, her head resting on white, embroidered pillows. Her now almost totally white hair – it had remained dark and glossy well into her old age – spread over them around her head. She looked very small and thin, her body covered with a colourful blanket. Her hands, very bent and wrinkled, her gold rings tight in the ends of her fingers, held fast by her swollen knuckles, she picked constantly at the wool bound edges of the blanket.

She looked up as Christina approached and a smile lit up her wrinkled old face. Christina took hold of one of her hands, stroking it gently and stilling the constant nervous movement of the fingers. They sat like this for a while, neither of them speaking, then Eleni finally, in a whisper, asked, "Where is the baby?" Ariadne who had been standing near, heard her and explained that they had not brought Lukas this time, he was being looked after by a friend in the village. Eleni shook her head but didn't say anything more and Ariadne left the room so that Christina could be alone with their grandmother.

"The baby, Christina, you had the baby?"

"Oh yes grandma, it was a boy but stillborn. He was so beautiful with fine blond hair. He is gone now."

Christina spoke quietly and without emotion though she felt as if her heart was breaking. Eleni returned the pressure of her granddaughter's hand.

"It was maybe for the best. And the father, Anthony wasn't it, you poor young people – the church so cruel."

"You guessed then grandma; yes I love him, we loved each other, but according to his vows we sinned." Christina fingered the small gold crucifix she wore around her neck, "This is all I have of him now." She didn't tell the old woman how the crucifix had come back into her possession. "He has gone away to Ireland, it's all over, finished."

Eleni closed her eyes, Christina waited for a little while but her grandmother had sunk into sleep so she pulled the coverlet up higher and smoothed it, then she tiptoed from the room.

News filtered through very slowly in the remote villages on the southern Irish coast, rumours circulated first in the meeting places, pubs, stores and post offices. They were discussed over pints of ale, at the ceilidhs, over the counters but only briefly, to be replaced by more important topics – the successes or failures of the local Gaelic football and hurling teams, the planned celebrations for the saints' days within the various parishes, equally as hotly debated and competitive as the sporting fixtures.

Anthony took little part in these local affairs. He lived out his solitary existence in his lodgings – kept clean and comfortable by his elderly landlady who would also cook meals for him when he wanted them. He spent his days walking on the shore or up in the hills behind it, observing the wildlife – the birds and the flowers, as he had the shells and little creatures that inhabited the rock pools on the shore long ago with Father Doherty, or reading; he had books from the library in the city sent to him at the post office which ran the beginnings of a mobile library for the village though the farmers and fishermen who lived and worked there had little time for books and reading. He didn't bother much with newspapers and listened very rarely to the crackling old radio in his room that his landlady had provided.

Gradually though, he had become aware of changes that were taking place within the priesthood that he had abandoned, guilty at having betrayed his faith and vows. There was talk of married Anglican priests being accepted into the Catholic Church after their argument with the rise of women in their ranks and possible changes regarding the matter of celibacy. Anthony began to take an interest in these developments and wondered if there would be a chance for him to be reunited with his love and that they could build a future together, somewhere in the world as young couples everywhere, not impeded by canonical strictures.

Meanwhile, in the Convent high above the village and the seashore beyond, Christina wrestled with her guilt; she still worked as a lay worker and was given more responsibility in her share of the daily tasks of running the farm that supplied the sisters with their daily needs of fruit and vegetables. Her long experience of the work since childhood on her parents' smallholding and her months of travelling and working with the growing infant within her, on the journey that had brought her here, put her in a good position to assist directly in organising the steady production of healthy, home-grown food.

She pondered the possibility of joining the novitiate and taking her vows, becoming a nun and devoting the rest of her life to the service of the order, but she couldn't revoke her feelings for Anthony. Were their actions really enough reason for her to cut herself off from the world? They had each in turn buried their child but Anthony had done so with the proper words of the church burial service to sanctify the tiny wayside grave. They had both repented and parted, surely that would gain them forgiveness.

Christina had spoken with some of the novices serving their initiation into the full vows required of them. The young girl who lain alongside her in the infirmary was steadfast in her decision, wanting to enlarge her religious studies and have greater access to the great history behind them. Another had been betrayed by her lover and sought refuge from any future relationships with the opposite sex, not an unusual reason for seeking seclusion in the convent – but Christina had neither of these reasons to justify her becoming a nun. She knew her grandmother, Eleni, had always believed that priests should be allowed to marry and old Father Giorgio had been sympathetic to that view. Surely it was the natural order of things that a priest could deal better with his congregation if he understood their problems as a husband and father himself. The title of Father indeed seemed a misnomer – at least Anthony really had deserved it.

Ariadne had made the journey up to the convent once or twice to visit her sister but they had not touched on what

Christina's plans were and kept their conversation to village
news and the fast growing up of Lukas.

Chapter Twelve

The worst of winter, the gales whipping up the waves in angry assault against the rocky shoreline, lashing rain and sometimes hail and even flurries of snow battering above them; overall leaden skies and the chill penetrating through one's bones, all these were finally giving way to a gentler tempo. Pale sunshine glinted on calmer seas, the waves breaking less fiercely on the edge of the strand, bare trees inland starting tentatively into leaf.

Anthony had struggled for months with his guilt in his lonely sojourn in the village with his feelings for Christina which were as strong as ever. He had gradually come to the decision that he must return to the island and face up to whatever was to come of his wayward actions. He still held to his faith but questioned the rules laid down for its practice. He prayed inwardly and constantly for some answers to his problems. Could he continue as an ordained priest in the light of his actions? He held to his belief that he had expiated his questionable sin of taking Christina and giving her his – their- child, his burial of the infant at the little rural wayside shrine was done with due care and appropriate blessing, more perhaps than would have been the case if his and Christina's relationship had been revealed, when an unmarked grave would probably have been the child's final resting place.

Ariadne had kept in touch with him occasionally and Anthony decided he would write to her and advise her that he intended to return. So far as he knew, Ariadne did not know anything of her sister's pregnancy and the reason for her living and working at the convent, the nuns who had taken her in must have been aware of her condition, so recently delivered of the child, but they kept the knowledge to themselves and respected her confidence – these women were more worldly than many people supposed.

Once he had made up his mind to go back, Anthony put his plans into action and began to make his travel arrangements. He had only briefly visited his family when he'd returned from the island to his homeland, not giving them any real explanation for his doing so and they had possibly accepted the he was on some sort of sabbatical; now he felt that he should see them again before he left, it would appear more normal, He would have to begin his journey from Dublin anyway, so maybe he could stay a few days there and catch up on family affairs before leaving.

Anthony was so glad he decided to go home first to his family. They welcomed him with such warmth. He watched his parents, noting how quietly happy they were with each other, his father reserved and shy, his mother the real centre of the home, busy all day with looking after everyone. His younger brother readily gave up his room to Anthony once again and enjoyed hearing more about the island and his life there. His mother fussed over him as usual, insisting on seeing to his packing, washing and ironing for him and replacing old clothes with new, he had to remind her that it would be very warm when he first got back to the island again and winter there was very mild compared to Ireland, he wouldn't need to take thick sweaters with him. Anthony wondered if she and his father would ever make the journey out themselves.

His mother was interested in whether he had any special friends among his congregation and wanted to know all about his young housekeeper who had replaced the older woman, Eleni.

Maura had begun teaching and now lived away from home, sharing a tiny flat with a colleague from the school in Killkenny a little way down the coast. There were only a couple of years between Anthony and his sister Maura, they had always been able to talk to each other and they shared views on all sorts of subjects. Maura had always been a good student through her school years, working conscientiously, leaning towards the academic side of her studies, she was destined to go to university and in due course had gained her place at Trinity College. She graduated with a good degree and had now started on her teaching career. She made time to meet up with Anthony on several occasions during the brief period he spent with their parents and the rest of the family, before he began his journey back to the island and whatever awaited him there.

Maura too had begun to question some of the tenets of the Catholic faith and had often expressed her views that priests should be allowed to marry and she listened to the vague rumours that were circulating at the time, discussing them with her brother.

If anyone was likely to go across the water and visit Anthony's island parish, it would be Maura and he and she talked of this happening in the sometime not too distant future, when Maura would have the long school summer vacation and would perhaps plan the trip with the friend who shared her flat. Anthony felt that Maura and Christina would like each other and he longed to introduce them and show Christina the real life Maura of the photographs she'd seen of his Irish family.

He had not spoken of Christina's existence to his sister, he had yet to untangle their troubled lives, their tragedy and their guilt and to make plans for their possible future together, though he had sometimes suggested to her that he would resign from the priesthood and take up some alternative career, perhaps – as Maura – in teaching.

Finally came the day for his departure and in a cool, misty Irish dawn, Anthony's plane rose into the sky and out over the Irish coast, he looked down through the thin cloud onto the rugged cliffs and breaking waves along the shoreline of his homeland. As the plane gained height, nosing up through the banked cloud, all that could be seen was infinite, vast blue sky. Anthony settle back in the seat, it would be the same clear, cloudless blue above the island Anthony thought and he prayed the same clarity of vision would show him the way forward to sharing his life with Christina.

Chapter Thirteen

The sun, high in the cloudless sky, burned down on the arid hillsides; tiny lizards scuttled beneath the scattered rocks, to laze in their shade until the evening cooled and they could stretch our once again on the weather-polished boulders and snap at and catch passing flies.

Far down beyond the greener valley floor, the sea lay calm and blue with sparkling pathways spreading out toward the distant horizon where blue sky and blue sea met in a misty line across the water. Other small islands punctuated the scene and the sails of boats moving between them patterned the water with their white wings. All this was visible from the convent garden where Christina rested, leaning on her hoe between the neat rows of vegetables she was tending. Her bare arms beneath the rolled back sleeves of her rough brown cotton habit, were deeply bronzed and her feet too in their practical sandals. Her long, dark hair was tied back off her face and tucked beneath a shady straw hat. She looked out across the garden and beyond down to the sea and wondered as she so often did, if Anthony ever looked across the cold, grey Irish water and thought of her. She fingered the little gold cross that she always wore on a chain round her neck and whispered his name under her breath, full of longing and regret. Then she turned back to her hoeing, there was an hour or two to go before the great bell rang for the next of the regular daily offices that she would attend. She had considered joining the order and becoming a novice but did she really want to go ahead with taking vows and reconciling herself to life with the nuns who had been so good to her? Mother Superior had urged the young woman to take time in making her decision, she feared that Christina had no real vocation for the convent life.

Christina felt so safe in these peaceful surroundings but she couldn't forget what had brought her here and the last hurried meeting with the young priest, Anthony. Nearly a year had gone by since then and her feelings for him were stronger than ever. What they had done was wrong but was it really so terrible? They were young like all the friends who had gathered around the fires on the beach, enjoying the barbecues and the fun, splashing in the water and singing along to the accompaniment of the bouzouki played by one of their number. Many of these young people who had paired off at the beach were now married and Christina envied them. Now she lived in this all female environment, the nuns' only contact with the opposite sex – other than rarely when they were teaching at the village school or helping new mothers with their babies – was when the priest came to hear their confession and the current one was a dour fellow, avoiding any social interchange with his congregation, not at all like Father Anthony, with his blond good looks and his happy laughter; many a heart had fluttered beneath their severe habits when he visited the sisters.

The bell began tolling and Christina wearily took her hoe and made her way to the shed where she propped it against the wall along with the other tools, after wiping it clean with the oily rag hanging there. She recalled there had never been time to clean the tools on the family smallholding where she had been brought up. She pulled off her hat and smoothing her hair, hurried towards the chapel, joining the novices to take their appointed places in the rear pews.

The chapel was so cool after the heat outside and Christina seated herself thankfully. She was tired after her day's work in the vegetable garden and she relaxed, letting the familiar sounds of the nuns chanting and singing, wash over her, revitalising her and dispersing the ache she felt in her back and shoulders from her efforts.

Christina bent her head in prayer and silently begged forgiveness for her sinning with Anthony and she prayed for the soul of their still-born baby. She was content the he had been decently buried with the proper Catholic rites said over his tiny body by his father and she found some comfort in this. She had had no time for bonding with her little son and maybe this eased her conscience as she retraced in her mind the painful walk through the hills to the convent, bleeding and exhausted.

The short service over, the older sisters retired to Mother Superior's sitting room for an hour of recreation and the others with novices and lay workers who had attended, went to the general common room before the simple supper was served, after which there would be an hour of religious studies before the final mass and they could retire to their allotted cells and hard, wooden cots.

As a lay worker, Christina had slept with the other women in the long dormitory beyond the garden but now she had been allowed her own private space in the Mother house and she had made it her own with photographs of her family and some simple religious ornaments. A bright, woven coverlet was spread over the narrow wooden bed – a gift from Ariadne, one of the photographs was of Ariadne's little boy, Christina's nephew, Lukas, now a smiling, healthy two-year-old.

Occasionally Ariadne made her way up to the convent to see her sister but these meetings were somewhat stilted as Ariadne could not know the reason for Christina's being there.

Despite her tiredness, Christina lay awake, stretched out in the plain white nightdress that she had been given, along with all the nuns, reviewing once again, as she did almost nightly, her situation and what was to be her future. All about was silent, only broken by the shrill cry of a night owl into the peace surrounding the ancient convent walls. Though she lay unmoving, Christina's brain kept working, turning over in her mind happy memories of the innocent days, keeping house for Anthony; the simple pleasure of picking fresh flowers to put in the vase on his breakfast table and preparing his favourite meals. She recited in her head the strange sounding names of his sisters back in Ireland and clutching at the little engraved cross that she never took off after it had been taken from her baby's tiny fingers and had found its way back to her from Anthony's hand through the grille of the confessional, she felt the longing for Anthony engulf her.

The 'fasten your seatbelt' sign came up and Anthony stretched his stiff limbs and fumbled for his belt. A stewardess walked up the aisle checking on her charges' compliance with the order, assisting and encouraging them. Anthony noted his neighbour holding the arm rest between them in a white-knuckled grip, her whole body was tense, her eyes screwed tightly closed. She had confided to him that she hated flying, especially take-off and landing. He leant across and covered her hand with his. He felt the change in the rhythm and cadence of the aircraft's engines as it began its slow descent through the wispy clouds and the first buildings of the airport below came into view far ahead. Minutes later they landed with a dull thud and scudded along the last few feet of the runway, the plane's tyres screeching as they came to a final, shuddering halt.

His travelling companion gave an audible sigh of relief and Anthony removed his hand from hers; she thanked him for his calming gesture and set about collecting her book and spectacles, putting them into her flight bag. Anthony reached up and got down both their coats from the overhead locker, they weren't going to need them now, the bright sunshine outside the cabin windows promised welcoming warmth.

The gang planks were swiftly wheeled into place against the fuselage and she joined the shuffling queue of passengers making their way to the exit. Anthony didn't rush to join them, he had no one meeting him but he knew that she had and didn't want to intrude. He watched her out of the window and saw her get aboard the shuttle bus to the arrivals area, he would get the next one and now made his own way out of the cabin, exchanging friendly farewells with the smiling stewardesses waiting either side of the exit. He saw his neighbour once more ahead of him in passport control – she smiled and waved and he waved back and then she was gone.

Anthony travelled light, just a haversack held all he wanted so he had no need to join the anxious throng looking out for their cases as they burst through the curtain onto the constantly circling belt in the cool, cavernous, luggage hall. He went straight out from going through the passport check into the blinding sunshine.

He planned to stay in the city for a couple of days, doing the tourist spots, the museums and ancient sites before he could arrange a ferry crossing from the port to the island – so now he had to find some accommodation. He tracked down an information office and Bureau de Change and got himself booked into a reasonably priced small bed and breakfast hotel in the city outskirts. The landlady, a buxom, friendly woman, showed him to his room on the second floor of the traditional white stucco house, it was plainly furnished but clean and comfortable, she was delighted that Anthony spoke her language and chattered away to him offering a meal if he should require it at once or later in the evening with her only other guest. Anthony settled for the latter, at the moment all he wanted was a good wash and change of shirt, the one he'd worn on the flight being damp with sweat and sticking uncomfortably to his back.